FAT FARM

FAT FARM

ALLEN CARTER

ISBN: 978-1-969865-73-2 (pb)
ISBN: 978-1-969865-74-9 (e)

Rev. date: 01/06/2026

CHAPTER 1

Amy smiled slightly to herself as her car crested the pass leading into the small mountain valley. The sign said, "Elevation 8,228 Feet." She had been over this road before a few times en route to Jackson Hole where she occasionally vacationed. It seemed like everybody else did as well. She was sort of amused that she was going through with this after all. She looked at it as a small adventure and hoped she would be glad she spent her time this way.

The road wound down a few switchbacks and came to the valley floor. Her mind wandered a little as she drove because the route was largely familiar, although she noticed a new log house here and there and livestock in the fields. A paint horse stood near the highway fence.

She thought, *One of these days I will get more serious about riding.* She hoped that these next few weeks would give her some opportunity to horseback ride in the majestic Rocky Mountains that towered on either side.

It seemed odd that her law firm would spend money this way on the employees, but she supposed that the return on their investment must be good, since they had continued their health-and-fitness program for three years now. She had actually delayed taking her allotted four weeks and six thousand dollars, which the attorneys called a health-and-fitness bonus, but which all the office staff referred to as "buns of gold." It was true that most of the younger attorneys and many of the paralegals and secretaries had done bigger adventures like biking in New England or rock climbing in Yosemite, but Sue, the secretary who was in Amy's cubicle and Bill, one of the paralegals, had both come here and had been quite satisfied with their experience. Amy didn't have nearly the amount of pounds to lose that either of them had, but since she wasn't much into rock climbing or marathon bicycling, she thought this would be an enjoyable way to fulfill the company policy and have some fun at the same time.

Oops! Better slow down, she thought, remembering the speeding ticket she got passing through this small town before. Population 385. She was well over the posted thirty-five mile-per-hour limit. Sure enough, there was the town cop car parked, empty, at the local cafe, so she pressed the accelerator since she was nearly at the other end of town already.

She tried to envision how her time might be spent and recalled that Sue had seemed a little vague about her day-to-day activities here, although Bill had recited a fairly interesting travelogue including mountain biking trips, horseback riding, a couple of days floating the river, along with morning calisthenics, and the usual fitness hoopla. Bill said he didn't even recollect eating much bad food, although there was the occasional All Bran milkshake, and it seemed like yogurt was in everything.

There it was, off to the right, fairly new construction, an interesting combination of A-framed log architecture with mortar and rock chimneys dotting the skyline amongst the many-directional dark green metal roof. As she turned into the large log gateway, the overhead beam read in typical rough Western engraving, Rocky Mountain Restoration Center. All in all, it was quite tastefully done, and although the campus buildings were impressively perched atop a hill at the base of a larger mountain, it struck her that for the numbers of people she knew that had been here, it was still relatively small. Her eyes couldn't help notice that on the slopes above the lodge, there were still considerable banks of snow despite the fact that it was early June. She stepped out of the car, noting that the air was much cooler than home, and it felt good as a light breeze tumbled down off the pines. A couple of joggers, equipped with sweat bands on every limb and on their heads, trotted by as she walked up the rock walkway; and she noticed that there was a large gravel parking area off below the lodge, sort of out of sight, where most of the cars were parked. She supposed she would need to move her little Honda coupe over there after she registered and wondered if she would be allowed to park it next to all the BMW, Mercedes, and Lexus vehicles arranged in tidy rows.

She entered the masculine log doorway into a lobby just like she had expected, complete with a rock fireplace, elk antlers, rustic log furniture and Cindy, a trim, five-four blond.

"Hi. You must be Amy. How was your drive?"

"It was really nice. No traffic here," she quipped, noticing as she stepped closer to Cindy that she appeared a little less petite and more muscular than at first glance. Amy tried to guess her age but wasn't sure she could even be within ten years.

"You can register right here at the desk," Cindy said. "And then I will show you to your bungalow. I'm Cindy. I manage the daily operations here, so we'll see quite a bit of each other, and I will be happy to help you with any concerns during your stay with us." Her tone was cordial but business-like.

Amy recollected that the center boasted bungalow living for the more affluent and dormitory-style quarters for those who wanted the budget plan, but since her firm had been a frequent customer and since this was actually still in what they considered their off season, they had offered her bungalow quarters at the discount price. A young man, probably a college student home for the summer, registered her, and Cindy led the way down the hall.

Amy mused to herself, So far this looks like a well-organized operation, as she walked out of the main lodge across a breezeway to the bungalows.

"Here you go," said Cindy. "You will be in number four."

Amy thought, I think Bill was in number four. She wondered if that was more than just coincidence and walked in. The quarters were modest and rustic but immaculately kept. It reminded her more of a high-end cabin in Yellowstone Park where she stayed on a family vacation in high school than a traditional motel room, particularly when she noticed there was no television, radio, or even telephone there. The interior walls were split log with white chinking, with white-painted window frames. Although there was a little closet, there were pegs protruding from the logs inside the door for hanging coats. The queen bed had a log frame and what looked to be a handtied quilt in a multicolored patchwork. Framed western scenes with landscapes and horses bedecked the walls here and there. Some leather and log chairs with brass nails snuggled a small table and lamp in the corner.

She noticed the door ajar to a clean white porcelain bathroom had a handle made of welded horse shoes. Most importantly, the horse shoes opened upward. Amy knew the folklore that horseshoes were lucky if turned up so the luck didn't run out.

Cindy said, "I hope this will suit you. You may recall from the materials we mailed you that we don't have TV or Internet because we don't want those distractions interfering with the intent and success of our program. There is no cell phone service here at the base of these mountains, and we prefer it that way. But there is a land line at the lodge you can use anytime. Pete will be glad to carry your bags to the bungalow, and we will move your car if you like."

Amy responded that she would go park it herself. "I would like to walk around the grounds a bit."

"That will be fine." Cindy smiled gently. "When you are ready, come find me and we will get started this afternoon."

"Thanks," Amy said and brushed her hair back as she walked by the mirror. She knew that they would ask her how many pounds she wanted to lose, and she hadn't quite made up her mind. She was not seriously overweight and thought that they might not have allowed her to come here except that she had such good rapport with her supervising attorney. It was true that the senior partners approved every health-and-fitness leave and had turned down a few of the employees, particularly secretaries, for a couple of their requests, apparently believing they were not sufficiently health-and-fitness oriented. It seemed like the paralegals and the lawyers almost always got their requests, and, of course, any of the firm's partners did what they wanted, no questions asked. It amazed her how much cash must roll through their law office to allow so many people such lavish expense accounts. That was one thing she liked about her employment. She had several friends who were also legal secretaries and who received little or no supplemental benefits, and here she was on an expensive four-week, resort-style, almost vacation on the company tab. Out the window, she could see Pete getting her baggage and thought she would go park her car. She met him coming up the walk to her room.

"Hi, I'm Pete!" He was late teens, maybe twenty, boyish, with sandy hair and drawly speech.

"I'm Amy. Nice to meet you."

"You're going to like it here! Ever been around here before?"

"I've driven through on the way to Jackson Hole." "Well, it's about time you stopped here first. This is better."

"It looks a lot like Jackson and the Tetons to me."

"No way-Jackson's too crowded anymore, people everywhere. Traffic and noise all the time."

Amy smiled at him, thinking that Jackson was where people from all over went specifically to get away from traffic, noise, and crowds.

"Funny, I've never thought of Jackson, Wyoming, as a crowded big city."

"Well, that's how it is turning out. And it's too bad." "Where are you from?" She had to try not to laugh or sound condescending.

"Here. Where else?" he blurted enthusiastically bouncing along, arms bulging with her luggage. "So what do you do for excitement around these parts?"

He didn't notice her contrived cowboy twang gently mimicking his just to see if he would even notice.

"We have rodeos, horse-pullin' matches, the fair, and every summer there's a canoe race on the river. My uncle won last year, and I'm in it this year an' I can win." By now he was following her back toward her car still carrying her bags.

"Let me take one of those, and I'll walk with you." She turned back toward her room.

"Okay." Not missing a beat, he turned around and kept talking." Plus, in the winter we've got great snowmobiling, and if I earn enough this summer, I'm building me a hill climber sled for the hill climbs." "I assume that's a snowmobile?"

"Yep, customized for low weight and power. You can win lots of money climbing."

She couldn't resist: "What about a college fund instead?"

"I've got two years till then, and Doc Fisher says if I do good, I can work here summers while I go to school to earn college money. He's a good guy, Doc Fisher, the best. Saved my grandpa when he had his heart attack. Well, here you go, see ya around." He set the luggage down and walked, waving, out the door-no pause for a tip, just a big smile and tousled hair disappearing down the path. She thought maybe that was the magic of it – simple pleasures, no hustle, no bustle. She already felt good here. Her mind drifted back home to Salt Lake City, her condo, a good job, friends—but they were mostly work friends. And Steve, how could she forget Steve? It was a relief to have it clearly over.

She wandered back through the main lodge, where she noticed an exercise room in the back. A couple of rather fit looking forty-year-old men trotted away on the treadmills, perspiration beading their foreheads.

As she got in her car, she thought to herself, I haven't seen anybody fat here yet. Her opinion changed instantly, though, as she looked in her rearview mirror. A new-looking Mercedes Benz pulled up, and a very roly-poly couple clambered out and headed into the lodge. She parked her car and went back to her bungalow, her stomach reminding her it was lunchtime. She entered the lodge in search of Cindy, whom she found greeting another couple a little less round than the last ones, but nevertheless, with plenty of weight to give. Amy wondered if she would be out of place.

Cindy motioned her to come over and said, "Amy, I would like you to meet Mr. and Mrs. James Herrett. They will be in our program along with you."

"Pleased to meet you," she said softly, feeling always a little shy around people older than her.

The couple smiled warmly and Jim extended his hand. He had on a pair of cut-off sweat pants, and Amy noticed vertical scars across both knees.

An ex-jock, she thought, not ever having had a great affinity for ball players in general, particularly the arrogant ones who lived across from her in college.

After the introduction, Cindy said, "Are you ready to get started?"

Amy responded affirmatively.

"Okay, let's go into my office."

The office was spacious and decorated with original watercolor paintings mostly of mountain scenes, one of which she recognized as the Grand Tetons. In the corner of each painting was the same set of initials, CB, which happened to match the initials on the monogrammed pen holder that sat on the desk.

"Do you paint?" asked Amy.

"Yes, I dabble in it as time permits. We have had some accomplished artists here, and I have taken the opportunity to pick their brains, you might say." She grinned. "Please have a seat."

Amy sat down. Cindy reached into her desk and pulled out Amy's file.

"Amy, we are truly pleased that you could come up and spend time with us. You are an attractive woman," she said, "and five years ago when we opened, I would have been surprised that someone like you wanted to come here. However, we have people of almost every size and description coming, all of whom seem quite satisfied." She went on, "For those who are not seriously overweight, we try to tailor the program a little more to conditioning and fitness rather than weight loss, but we will approach this any way you like. Let me ask you a few questions." She got right to the point. "How much weight do you want to lose?"

Amy responded, "Maybe fifteen pounds. Or eighteen would be best. I might regain a little bit after the program. I've done that before when I diet."

Cindy explained, "The intent of our process here is to help our clients lose and then maintain their weight loss." She went on, "We have found if people anticipate regaining a little, that they tend to regain a lot when they go home and those who plan to hold the line, do a lot better, but you can do it anyway you like." She smiled.

The list of questions continued about favorite activities and Amy, of course, mentioned horseback riding as one of them. She was surprised at the variety of options available and the seeming flexibility in scheduling her days. She wondered how they could keep track of everybody if everyone was on such an individual program. She had expected a whole lot more group activities. She tried to remember how Bill and Sue had organized their month, and found her recollection to be not very detailed.

Cindy brought her attention back when she said, "We have an on-campus photographer who will take a few pictures of the goings-on around here from time to time. I am sure you recall when you signed up that we will provide you any photographs that you like for your photo album. If you would be willing to allow us to use some of these photos in our promotional materials, please initial this form right here."

She initialed as she said, "Can I change my mind later?"

"Oh sure, we would never print anything that would make any of our clients uncomfortable." She looked rather serious. "We observe absolutely strict confidentiality rules around here." Then she smiled again graciously. "I will take you to the cafeteria for lunch, and you can meet some of the other clients. We have you scheduled to confer with Dr. Fisher at two o'clock, and I will show you where his office is on the way." She promptly stood up and led Amy out of the room, down the hall on the other side of the lobby and into a typical cafeteria-style dining room. Sure enough, they had yogurt there.

Cindy introduced Amy to Nora, the cook, and said, "Nora will know you by name and will help you with food selection as soon as you and Dr. Fisher have designed a diet program this afternoon."

There were only a few people in the dining room. Jim and Maggie Herrett, she recognized. Cindy introduced her to Bert and Cathy Peterson and Norm and Jacqueline Blake whom she sat with to eat. On the opposite side of the dining room, there were two men in their late thirties, who all in all, despite being a little bit plump, were both pretty handsome, she thought.

She liked the dark-haired one more and was tempted to go sit down by them but hadn't quite had the nerve. It turned out the Herretts were from a town in central Washington she had never heard of and the Blakes and the Petersons were both from Salt Lake City and actually had come up together.

Lunch was good, if a little sparse, and she managed to eat nothing that contained yogurt for her first meal. She smiled to herself. I better call Bill and tell him I made it a whole day without yogurt here.

At two o'clock, she stood in the doorway of Dr. Fisher's office. He looked up from his desk, smiled, and said, "Hi, Amy. Come in and sit down." He stood and extended his hand. She noticed he was a balding man. She assumed in his early forties, but he looked remarkably fit and comfortable compared to most of the doctors she knew. She had understood before she registered that this was a legitimate enterprise and that he was a true M.D., unlike many self-proclaimed fitness experts; and, sure enough, there on the wall, was a diploma from the

University of Washington School of Medicine and a bunch of other framed diploma-looking documents like every doctor, dentist, and veterinarian seems to have. She thought, *Washington, that probably explains the Herretts coming so far.*

Dr. Fisher sat down in his chair, smiled again, and said, "We are pretty informal around here, so you can call me Dr. Fisher if you like, but most people just call me Doc, and a few call me Robert. We are very pleased to have you spend a month with us, and we are sure you won't be sorry. I have reviewed your file and the medical records your family physician provided us." He grinned. "I wish every patient I had here was in as good health and condition as you are. My job would be pretty easy." He continued, "I will just let you know that your firm has paid in advance for your stay, so everything is taken care of in that regard, and you don't need to worry about any financial matters. That will allow us to simply get down to business."

The next hour was spent with a series of standard medical questions with fairly detailed inquiry about eating habits. Dr. Fisher moved right along in a businesslike fashion through his forms, checking the appropriate boxes. He spent considerable time asking about any medications she had used in the past, any side effects or allergies she might have experienced and asked an awful lot of questions about a laparoscopic surgery she had for a cyst on an ovary a few years prior. Amy had understood that this was a pretty routine procedure, and although she remembered being fairly sore for a few days, she had not thought much about it since as her gynecologist had told her all went well and she should have no further problems.

The whole exercise took about an hour, after which he stood and said, "If you will kindly step with me across the hall into my examination room, Carol will take some vital signs, and I will do a brief physical examination."

Amy had kind of forgotten that a physical exam was part of the deal, but it certainly came rapidly back to her memory when he mentioned it, and she determined to go along. As it turned out, it was a fairly brief, painless exam with the usual look in ears and throat and listen to heart sort of thing. Dr. Fisher spent most of the time chatting away as he examined her and it set her at ease.

Having completed that, he jotted a few notes in the folder he held. "We will do a few blood tests this afternoon, then Paula will take you around the facility, so you know where to be for the various activities we plan in the morning. We will provide you a personalized schedule for your month here." Tucking his pen into the pocket of his blue denim shirt, he continued, "If you approve, then we will get started. I am confident you will walk out of our program slimmer, physically fit, and happy." He grinned again and walked out of the room.

Amy stepped behind a small curtain, and put on her clothes. Just as she was buttoning up her shirt, there was a tap on the door. It opened, and in walked Paula, who moved like she might bubble over at any moment. "Come on, Amy," she said tossing her head. "Let's go have some fun," and out the door she went with Amy struggling to keep up, still tying her shoe.

Paula took her around to a surprising array of activity bases, as she called them. There was a stable and corrals, but no horses there. When Amy inquired about horses, Paula said, "We lease them from the Welch Ranch down the road, and so they only bring them up certain days. That keeps us from having to do so much horse wrangling, and frankly, it keeps it smelling better around here. Would you have gotten out of your car if it smelled like a dairy?" She laughed without waiting for a response and was already walking off.

They went by another little log outbuilding, with the characteristic forest-green metal roof containing an assortment of mountain bikes in various sizes and colors. Paula reached in her fanny pack and pulled out a measuring tape, bent down, and measured Amy's inseam so abruptly that she almost jumped back.

"You will need a fifteen-inch-frame bike," Paula said and made a note of it on a little pad she was carrying. "Come on, Amy. We've got more to see," she said and away they went. At the end of their little campus tour, they had caught up with the Herretts, the Petersons, and the two men Amy had looked over in the cafeteria.

Paula said, "Have you met everyone?" Amy shook her head no and glanced in the direction of the two men. "Oh, this is David, and this is Thomas," she said. "They are both in the oil business in Billings, Montana."

"Pleased to make your acquaintance," said Amy. David was the dark-headed one. She had always been partial to dark headed men.

It was then time for a little stroll around the nature trail with Paula, who took off at a brisk pace, and everyone else fell in. Amy ended up walking with the Herretts with whom she was fairly comfortable already. Maggie, who was a few years older, had a kind, motherly disposition that led Amy to gravitate with her along the nature trail. Paula was pointing out plants and flowers and talking about their taxonomy and medicinal uses, but she was far enough ahead of the group that no one caught the entire recital, and, in fact, everybody was sort of chatting quietly among themselves getting acquainted. Amy had hoped for a few more younger, single people, but thought to herself, What do you expect at a fat farm? Soon, everyone was picking up the pace a little bit to keep up with Paula, and she noticed Jim Herrett favoring one knee.

By suppertime, everyone was pretty comfortable with each other and after a tasteful but rather sparse meal, they gathered around the fire place in the lobby of the lodge with Cindy.

Thomas said, "Cindy, there are lots of cars and not many people; where is everybody?"

Cindy smiled that usual warm smile, and said, "Well, not everybody is here right now. You will spend several days out at some of our satellite cabins, depending on the program you set up. Right now, we have a group on the Snake River who will be back Thursday about mid-day. You will probably get to meet some of them then."

The evening was spent in a nutrition and exercise slide presentation. It struck Amy as being a little bit simplistic, but like everything else, it was upbeat and well organized.

CHAPTER 2

The next morning, Paula tapped on the cabin doors to make sure everybody was awake and rounded the little group up for breakfast. Dr. Fisher met with them in the cafeteria. He gave another little speech. By now, Amy was wondering, When do we get on the mountain bikes or go do something? She felt a lot more like she was in school than a fitness center. Still, it was hard to argue with the friendly, personal disposition of the staff toward her and the others.

Dr. Fisher announced, "We will have a hypnotist in who will see you from time to time. His name is Carl; he has a master's degree in fitness psychology, and he will meet you individually this morning. While that is going on, I will be firming up a schedule with each one of you and discussing the results of your blood testing we did yesterday afternoon."

Amy's morning was spent going over her blood tests, which were normal, and setting up her schedule, which included sort of a general mix of all the activities that they had available, except that Amy had opted for no rock climbing. She considered that more dangerous than fun and had no particular interest in trying it.

She used the phone in the lodge to call her mom. "Hi, Mom, just calling to let you know I made it to this retreat okay. How are you and dad doing?"

"We're fine. Your father is getting new sod for the back lawn. He thinks the grass is too bumpy back there. You know how he is. What's it like there?"

Amy answered, "It's actually really nice; everybody is friendly, and it's beautiful and quiet."

"Any cute guys?"

"Geez Mom! Is that all you think about? Well, maybe one or two. Remember it's a weight loss thing, you know."

"I just want you to be happy, honey."

"I am happy, Mother. I gotta go. I don't have any cell service here, so I'm going to call Pam too. I just wanted to let you know I'm here and fine."

Pamela answered the phone, "Hey sis, what's up?"

"Just saying hi from the Rocky Mountain Restoration Center," she said with emphasis and went on, "way up in the boonies. It's pretty cool here. I'm going riding today!"

"You're psyched up about that aren't you?"

"Sure I am. You would be too. We're mountain riding, I think. The lodge is right against the hills." "Cool. Maybe I should drive down and see you while you're this close."

"That would be fun. I don't know exactly when to say, because they have us scheduled out 24/7. But I'll check and call you back. Only landlines here."

"Okay, let me know."

"All right. I have an appointment so I have to run. Love ya."

Then there was the meeting with Carl, the psychologist. Amy thought that he was classic and that if she had sketched a picture of a hypnotist it would look just like Carl. He had a high forehead with furrows, round wire-rimmed glasses, and what beard his narrow face could muster. The whiskers were sparse but tapered to a point at his chin.

"So, Amy," he said, "we have a little evaluation to do to see if hypnosis can help you reach your goals here. I have a few questions for you that may seem a little odd, but just answer as best you can. This won't take too long."

He reached in his desk drawer, pulling out a stopwatch, which he laid on the desk, and continued, "I would like you to remember three things while we talk that I will ask you later. The three things are an apple, a table, and a boot. Have you got them?"

She nodded.

He continued, "Can you tell me about any dreams you had last night?"

She pursed her lips as she thought about it. "I guess I don't remember much right now. I mean, I usually have dreams, I suppose, but on the spot I can't really think of them. Is that bad?"

"That is actually quite normal, but people vary a bit. There really isn't a right or wrong answer."

"That's good," she said looking momentarily off in the distance.

"Now if you can, start at one hundred and count backward by seven as far as you can go."

Amy made it to seventy-two then hesitated, "Umm. Sixty-five."

Carl stopped her, "That's fine to there. It's more difficult than you expect, isn't it?" His face didn't show much emotion as he went on, "Now can you recite the pledge of allegiance?"

"Whew, it's been a while but I think so." And she did.

"Thank you, Amy. Now I would like you to untie your left shoe first, then untie the right. Then retie them, right shoe first as quickly as you can."

"Very good," Carl said nodding. "Now can you remember the three things?"

After a momentary stall she said, "An apple, table, and a um, boot, right?"

"That's correct."

"Man, that was a little harder than I thought," she said eyebrows rising.

"Yes, it is. But you did fine. I think we will have no problem." With that he stood and excused her out of the room, inviting in Jackie Blake as Amy went out.

By afternoon, a rattly pickup truck and large horse trailer pulled in and unloaded some stocky, docile horses into the corral. Amy, the Herretts, and the Petersons met at the corral where a handsome, muscular cowboy was saddling a dun-colored mare that looked over her shoulder at the arriving guests as if the horse were choosing the rider instead of vice versa. Amy leaned her elbows over the log corral's top rail. A sorrel brown horse with white socks on both hind feet came up and sniffed her forearm. She patted his nose and looked at her reflection in his deep-brown eyes.

"You like him?" Lawrence called across the corral.

"Uh huh," she returned.

"His name is Easy Boy. He thinks he's people," the cowboy continued. "A little lazy, but gentle and smart. Watch him, or he'll taste all that pretty hair you got." "Okay. Can I ride him today?"

"Sure can. We'll saddle him next." He came toward her with a brush.

"Hi, folks. I'm Lawrence. It's a good day for a ride." He pushed his black cowboy hat up off his face with his index finger, exposing a ruddy complexion with deep lateral eye creases and two days' stubble of a beard. A blue bandana wrapped his neck under his snap-fronted paisley western shirt collar. He shook hands across the fence with each of the group and started to brush down Easy Boy.

"I'll brush him," Amy said, already halfway over the fence. "Is it okay?"

"Sure thing. Do you know horses?"

"Just a little."

"Talk to him when you walk behind." He slipped a halter over the gelding's head and draped the lead rope over the rail pole.

Amy brushed the dust off his back and stroked his neck with her free hand. The earthy smell of horses made her feel like Annie Oakley.

Lawrence returned with saddle and blanket, the dragging cinch kicking up little swirls of dust around his worn boots.

"Nice job you're hired, wrangler and rodeo queen," he quipped.

"Thanks, I guess." She smiled back.

"Want to saddle him, too?" "Yeah, I'll try."

"Nothing to it." He handed her the blanket, and she placed it over Easy Boy's back.

"Slant it just a little more forward than you want," he said, shifting the pad ahead. "Then you throw on your saddle and slop the whole thing back an inch. That smoothes his hair back so he won't get sores."

Amy was already lifting the saddle off the rail but struggled slightly with its weight and awkwardness. Lawrence added an assist, and the saddle plopped in place.

"If you want to cinch him, I'll go saddle the rest."

"Okay." She already was reaching under his belly for the cinch strap, surprised at her own eagerness since she'd only done this a time or two before, but it was fun. Simple pleasure from simple things, she thought again, just like Pete the luggage boy. She patted the horse.

By the time she'd fastened the cinch and breast collar, Lawrence had saddled the remaining two horses for the group, and returned with a bridle for hers. "My, you're fast," she teased.

"Practice, practice, practice." He had a Western drawl, and Amy expected him to say "ma'am" after everything.

By now, Maggie Herrett had followed Amy's lead and come into the corral.

Cathy Peterson, leaning through the rails, called, "Can I ride the gray one?"

"You bet," the cowboy replied.

Amy noticed Jim and Bert pointing at a saddle and chatting on the other side of the corral.

Lawrence adjusted Amy's stirrups longer.

"My girls have been riding this saddle, so it's too short," he explained. "How tall are you? Five-five?" "About that, yes."

He deftly set the stirrups and then helped her and the others into their seats. Jim's bad knees and big size created a momentary challenge in mounting since he had a tall black horse, but he muscled his leg over its back and was on.

Amy was looking forward to this. She liked Easy Boy. She appreciated the genuine manner of the people here, like Lawrence, who led the way out of the corral and up the trail into the mountains behind the lodge.

The horses were so docile that the ride might have been monotonous except for the fabulous scenery present on all sides as they wound single file up a steep sided canyon and out onto a rocky ridge that then led up to a higher, pine-covered mountain. The horses were stepping through edges of snow banks part of the way, and Amy was glad that they had reminded her to bring her jacket. By late afternoon, they were unbelievably high. The lodge could be seen as a small, indistinct structure below, and the entire valley floor was visible with a ribbon of highway winding its way along the glistening river that followed it back to the south where Amy had driven over the pass the day before.

Cathy twisted in her saddle facing Amy behind her. "Is this gorgeous or what?"

Amy nodded vigorously.

From behind her Maggie answered, "It's kind of scary it's so steep up here. But it is so scenic."

Calm was disrupted, however, when a mule deer burst from the trees ahead of them and bounded down the bare slope into some chokecherry and aspen below. Lawrence stopped his horse and turned around to the others, pointing out that the doe allowed them so close because she undoubtedly had a fawn hidden in the trees. Cathy Peterson inquired if they could go look for the fawn.

Lawrence discouraged it, saying, "The survival of these newborn deer depends upon their being left alone. We should move along so the mother can return to her baby." He lowered his cowboy hat slightly, turned the buckskin gelding he rode around and started back up the trail. Amy could tell he was a real cowboy, not the dime-store type who frequented the Western bars in Salt Lake but who probably never had touched a saddle. It was common out West to see these sorts in their pickup trucks with the gun rack in the back window filling the whole cab space with the width of their cowboy hats, driving up and down the road. She had always been amused at the self-important air put on by these characters she considered rather comical. The horses started down on the shady side of the canyon, and the trail entered the pine trees. It was quiet, quite cool, and dim as they worked their way down, hooves kicking the soft layer of pine needles ahead of them. As the horses came out of the trees, she was alarmed by a clicking sound and looked over to see someone standing just above the trail, snapping pictures with a great big lens protruding from his camera.

The camera lowered, and a bearded face behind it said, "Hi, I'm Ted. I'm the photographer you've heard about, just taking a few pictures. Hope you're enjoying your ride."

Amy thought, How in the world did he get up here? But her eye quickly caught the brown form of a horse tied to a pine tree a few yards above the trail, tail swishing and saddle bags bulging with tripods and other camera paraphernalia.

Ted rode with them back to the lodge. By then it was time to clean up and meet for a late supper. The Blakes and Thomas and David joined the group then, jabbering on about the fish they had caught that day on a river float trip.

Amy slumped into bed that night, surprised at how tired she was from riding.

CHAPTER 3

The next morning, Amy awoke feeling refreshed and invigorated. She thought time away from work with recreational activities in this serene mountain setting was going to be good for her, and she was glad she had come. She sat with Thomas and Dave for breakfast and chatted casually about nothing. Dave appealed to her somewhat, so she directed most of her attention at him. She wasn't sure he was exactly her type but figured that she might as well be friendly since they would be spending time together anyway and thought she might enjoy his company over the next few weeks. He was a little too confident and full of himself but had dark, penetrating eyes and seemed to be intelligent. He was also quite complimentary to Amy, and she thought maybe he liked her too. Thomas, on the other hand, had a personality that was a little sharper around the edges, and she didn't find herself as comfortable with him.

As she left the table, she realized that Thomas and Dave had reminded her of Steve. It had been a two year off-again, on-again relationship. He was a fine guy, a truly good person, successful in his business, but he made everything so complicated. It had exhausted her by the end, but she cared about him and had hung in there. Neither had been comfortable enough to commit to anything more, so when he had to move his business to Phoenix, an end was declared to the relationship by default. It was a relief to Amy at least; and probably to him. She just didn't have the heart to hurt him, and there was no good reason to stop seeing each other, so things had dragged on. She had wished she could find some fire in his soul, but he lacked something, somehow substituting analytical evaluation for passion.

In the end, geography made a clearer decision than either of them had been able. She wondered why she had persisted with Steve with no clear end in sight. Probably the same reason she used to go see Mr. Hillyard when she was a little girl. Mr. Hillyard, the eccentric old man at the end of the street. Her mom would say, "You girls take this bread down to Mr. Hillyard; he doesn't get out much."

So she and Pamela would start out for old man Hillyard's, but after the first few times, Pamela wanted to throw the bread in the neighbor's hedge and just tell Mom they'd been. "She'll never know, Amy. Come on. Throw it in the bushes."

But Amy couldn't do it. She had to deliver the bread. Old man Hillyard would invite them in. He wasn't really scary, just cantankerous. He'd grumble about this or that a while, then send the girls home without even a thank you or a smile.

Soon, Pam would say, "I'm not going. You go and don't tell Mom, or I'll get you."

Coaxing didn't work, so Amy usually went alone – the dutiful sister.

She had to smile to herself, maybe she and Steve had deserved each other, he the analyzer, she the dutiful plodder. Still, she felt a freeness to be out of the relationship. She had a little sense of adventure now – not a lot by some standards, but for Amy, pretty good. Now, here she was in the Wyoming Rockies, granted at a health club for overweight people, but it was a start away from dull and dutiful.

Amy walked out onto the deck in front of the lodge. The morning sun fell across her, and it felt great. A pair of ducks wheeled by in the sky overhead and angled away from the lodge, dropping altitude as they went toward the river bottom. Cindy stepped out on the deck behind Amy and said, "The ducks are beautiful. In a few more weeks, we will have mother ducks and baby ducks waddling across the lawn as they come up from the river." Cindy really seemed to be the genuine article. She fit in perfectly in this environment, but somehow Amy still thought this woman was too fault free to be real. Her blond hair, cut crisply at her shoulder, illuminated by the sunlight, accentuated her green eyes and that ever-present gentle smile. She liked her but wouldn't exactly say that she trusted her.

Cindy said, "You're first for the hypnotism session this morning, Amy. I am sure you will find it quite comfortable. We have found hypnotism allows our clients to incorporate and assimilate the things that they learn here so much better. Since we started it, we've had a marked reduction in the relapse rate of our customers." She continued, "We also have noticed much higher client satisfaction since we have had Carl as part of our team."

"How do you know people are more satisfied?"

"Oh, we will have you fill out a fairly extensive evaluation at the end of the program," Cindy replied. "We are constantly trying to improve and want feedback. After all, it is your happiness and sense of well-being we are really wanting to affect. Besides," she joked, "if you want your car keys back, you have to fill out the form."

Amy mentioned that her sister might like to come up and visit. Cindy responded quite abruptly to her inquiry, polite as always, but she said, "We seriously discourage visitors. This is a closed campus, and we find family visits to be highly disruptive and negatively influence our long-term outcomes. Oh sure, we have had family members visit from time to time, but largely, we request that you avoid it. If she really wants to come over, then have her come the last few days that you will be here, and we will adjust your schedule so you can spend time with her. Do you feel all right about that?"

"I guess so." Amy responded thinking to herself, I signed up for a health club not reform school. Still, it was hard to argue with Cindy's logic and her always polite manner.

Cindy put her hand on Amy's shoulder and said, "Come on. Let's go find Carl. You will like this. It will be fun." And they walked back into the lodge.

Amy sat across the room from Carl in a large, overstuffed chair. His office had three doors. How perfect. A psychologist with an office with door number one, door number two, and door number three. She seemed to hear so much about multiple personality patients and figured maybe if they came in his office with one personality, then they could go out another door if they were somebody else by the end of the session. There was no couch in the office, but the overstuffed chair was similar enough that she couldn't help wondering if she'd have inkblots to look at later. Carl walked around from his desk and reached in his pocket. She fully expected him to pull out a gold watch on a chain and start swinging it. Instead, out of his pocket came a small card with a series of numbers on it.

"Amy," he said, "I would like you to begin the session by memorizing a series of numbers. I will give you a few minutes to look over this card, and then ask you to recite these back to me."

Amy was quick with letters and numbers because of her legal secretary occupation, and shortly had the series learned, repeating them to Carl. This exercise was followed by several other mundane memory chores and some relaxation talk by Carl about relaxing her toes, feet, knees, etc. Amy relaxed and almost fell asleep, even though it was early in the day and she had slept well the night before.

She thought, I forgot to call Pam. I will need to do that later, and Carl asked her to please concentrate on relaxing. His office wall paper had a pale beige stripe in it.

CHAPTER 4

Amy groaned. Her head hurt. It was dark and kind of cold. She had been having a bizarre dream about running through a grocery store looking for low-fat foods. She tried to wake herself up and clear her mind, but she continued to feel drowsy like she couldn't move. She went to reach for the quilt because she was cold, but her hand wouldn't move. Still in a daze, she tried again. Again, her hand didn't budge. She squinted, opened her eyes wider, but it was pitch black. She then realized that she was damp down her right side from her hand down along her thigh. By now, she was alarmed and tried to call out but could hardly coordinate her efforts, so she sort of moaned. Again, she struggled to bring a hand up to her face and couldn't do it. She attempted to move her feet, or roll and found herself restrained. She struggled to stay alert and to speak or yell, but still couldn't manage it.

She took a couple of deep breaths and thought, *Calm down, and figure out what's wrong here.* She tried again to see something and rolled her head over to the side. Vaguely she could make out the reflection of a metallic pole standing beside her and then caught the glint of light off glass and plastic tubing. It took a moment, but she recognized this as an IV set. *Oh no, I am in a hospital,* she thought. *What happened to me?* She tried to recollect how she got there and could not. I must have been in an accident, she thought, now panicky.

Okay, I am in a hospital. I am sick or hurt, and I need to get my bearings. She struggled again to look around her but could barely see anything. She pulled with her arms but both were restrained at the wrist; her feet also. She stared into the darkness further. No nurse call button, no light, no window, no bedside table, no nothing.

She was, again, tempted to scream for help, but somehow, something told her to try to gather her wits. She seemed to be waking up a little better now, so she just lay still. Finally her eyes began to focus, and she wasn't sure whether she could see or just feel water trickling down along her side. No wonder she was cold, she was wet and so was the bed sheet. She remembered nothing except the events of the previous day. It must clearly be night, however, because it was so dark everywhere. She struggled to free her left hand, and with much pulling and twisting, it slipped free of whatever was holding it. She reached quickly across to the other side and her fingers grasped IV tubing, which was wet. As the moisture trickled down her fingers, she thought, My gosh, I'm bleeding, but then realized that it was running out the end of the plastic IV tubing. She was more or less alert now. She began to struggle to free her other hand and thought she would yell for help when she heard voices. Just as she inhaled to scream, she recognized the voice. It was Cindy.

Her tone was entirely different, and she was saying, "You have to keep them deep enough that they have no spontaneous movement." The voice was coming closer and suddenly seemed almost next to her. Instead of screaming, Amy shoved her left-hand back down into whatever had been restraining it.

"Damn," came Cindy's voice again. "The line is disconnected."

Amy quickly felt hands on her, picking up the IV tubing and manipulating it somewhere in the area of her right wrist.

Again something told Amy not to cry out. A light came on dimly at that moment, and she squinted. It was Cindy muttering harshly and connecting the IV line again. There was another figure in the room that she didn't recognize. The whole feel of it all was so sinister that Amy was terrified. She held absolutely still, squinting her eyes nearly shut, like a child trying to fool her parents into believing she is asleep. Cindy said something about tape and the other figure answered something. Amy could tell it was a man's voice but could not understand what was being said. As quickly as it all began, both people departed, and it was again dark.

Amy was keenly aware that something was seriously wrong with this situation. She instinctively knew that she needed to disconnect the IV. She wiggled her left hand free again, reached across, found the tubing and pulled. Tape tore away from her arm and she could feel something glide out from under her skin. She fumbled rapidly with the other wrist and found a buckled strap across it. It was awkward with her left hand, but only took moments to undo the buckle. Both hands were free, and she recognized that both feet were similarly restrained. A wave of drowsiness came over her, but she fought it, managing to sit up in bed. She was covered with a thin blanket and the sheet under her was damp. She shivered.

Rapidly, she worked to free her feet. She realized then that she was dressed only in a flimsy smock. A hospital gown, she thought, maybe I am in a hospital. Nevertheless, something inside told her to be careful. She crawled out of the bed and fell to the floor. Her muscles were so weak, and she felt so otherworldly stiff. She could barely bend her knees or reach out to catch herself as she slipped down. The floor was hard and icy cold.

Struggling to stay in control, she crawled along, feeling her way. She was still not fully alert but enough so to feel a tube dangling between her legs. Her hands explored in the dark, and she recognized it as a catheter. This was familiar because when her sister had surgery, Amy had been in the room when the nurse had placed a bladder catheter. She tugged on it and felt pain inside. The discomfort roused her further as panic set in, and she yanked on the tube again. The pain made her slump right onto the floor but was only momentary, and just as quickly, she was back up on her hands and knees feeling her way. Her hands met a junction of wall and floor. She slid them up along the wall and attempted to stand. At first, she could not make her feet work. She fought the overwhelming urge to yell for help and forced herself to an upright position. Her knees tended to buckle; she could barely stand. Again, she was conscious of voices and froze absolutely still.

The man's voice first said, "If we drop the temperature three more degrees, I think we can raise weight loss ten percent."

Cindy's voice was next. "You're pressing your luck. If we lose somebody, we're finished."

Amy stood, shivered, wanting to cry. The voices retreated, and she felt her way along the wall finding a door jam, feeling for a latch. She still struggled to maintain her balance and had to stay against the wall. There it was, the door handle. She pushed the lever quietly. As the door opened, some light entered the room. Her eyes, fully dark adapted, caught a stark vision of where she was with the little light that entered the crack in the door. Walls, floor, were cement. There was a small cot or bed with an IV pole she had been attached to. Nylon webbing with buckles had strapped her to the bed. A set of headphones dangled from the cot. Some electrical conduit ran across the ceiling and save for that, there was nothing else in the room, but the IV pole and bag of liquid. The bladder catheter lay on the floor attached to a bag, liquid spilled from it. In the darkness, she couldn't make out whether it was urine, blood, or what.

By now, Amy's mind was in full self-preservation mode. She slipped through the open doorway into a dimly lit corridor. She shivered again. Her legs could barely carry her, and her knees were chafed from crawling across the cement. She could see a series of doorways. She slipped along the wall to the first one, took a deep breath, and then eased open the latch. As the light fell across the room, she saw the exact vision of where she had just been, except that someone was in the cot. She recognized the dark hair immediately. It was Dave.

The impulse to scream was overwhelming, but by now, she knew better. She closed the door and had presence of mind to go back and close the door where she had been. She could not resist opening another doorway, which was across the narrow corridor. Sure enough, a concrete cubicle, a body in a bed with an IV attached to it. She knew she had to get out. Down the corridor, she stumbled, struggling to maintain an upright status. Her hands reached down along her thighs as she tried to walk, and the body that they contacted felt unfamiliar. It was she, all right, but definitely thinner, stiff in all of her joints and stumbling. By the end of the corridor, the illumination was a little better and stairs led up. Had she comprehended the entire risk, she would probably never have dared climb them, nevertheless, she was fleeing, and although her body could only accomplish it slowly, her mind was at full speed.

CHAPTER 5

The door at the top of the stairs was commercial grade metal but unlocked. Amy carefully eased it open and recognized a finished hallway complete with light fixtures and wall hangings. Her first impression was to shrink back from it, but suddenly the voices of Cindy and her companion were behind her. She had no choice but to slip through it. The hallway was vacant. By now, she could stumble along a little faster as her joints limbered, and she hurried along it, not knowing where she was going. It was soon apparent that she was in the lodge. A few feet behind her, the voices entered the stairwell she had just come out of. She forced her legs to take bigger steps and saw another doorway ahead. At this one there was no hesitation. She opened it, virtually falling through it, terrified now of being caught. She stumbled, slipped, and rolled.

She was rolling in grass. She was outside.

It was dim and very cold. She tried to get to her feet, failed twice, but succeeded on the third attempt, getting away from the building and toward some sheltering trees nearby. She collapsed behind the hedgerow and tried to get her bearings, breathing heavily.

She knelt, looked around, and recognized the campus, outside the lodge. At first she wasn't sure whether it was morning or evening. As her gaze caught the parking lot, lodge, and the bungalows, however, she recognized a brighter sky in the west and realized that it was dusk. Her mind raced. She was outside, freezing, essentially naked, horribly weak with stiff joints, and it was nightfall. Her thoughts immediately went to her car. She knew where it was but needed keys and clothes. Bungalow number 4, her mind was fully active now. She stayed in the cover of the surrounding vegetation moving toward the bungalows.

By now, she knew exactly where she was on the campus and came up behind her cabin. A sense of relief came over her, and she went along the side of the building around toward the front door. As she came along the window, however, she noticed lights on and people inside. She stopped short, holding her body away from the window and peered inside. These were strangers. Furthermore, nothing in the place was familiar. The jackets on the hat stand were different, and it was not her purse on the table. She jerked back from the window, her back hitting against the cabin wall.

A voice said, "Did you hear something?" "Hear what?" a man's voice responded.

"I heard a thump outside. Go see what it is." "It's just a little forest critter. Let's get unpacked. Did you bring any munchies?"

"No, go see what it is. What if it is a bear?"

"Yeah, right, a bear."

"No snacks until you go check."

"Okay, okay."

A rotund man came out of the cabin. Amy slid down the wall and froze. The man gave a cursory glance around the side of the building and turned to go back in.

"No bear. Where's those chips?"

Amy had a strong urge to call out and follow him into the light. It was then the horrifying thought occurred to her that she had been in whatever that basement was, for at least a fair period of time and that to enter the bungalow would mean being found out. *Am I having some paranoid psychotic experience? Whatever's going on, I can't be discovered.* She slipped back into the choke cherry behind the cabin. Tears of confusion welled up in her eyes.

She tried to think of any nearby buildings or anything she could get to. She remembered the long gravel lane leading to the Rocky Mountain Center. It had to have been nearly a mile long and she could barely walk and was freezing.

The horses, she thought suddenly and was instantly making her way to the stable. "Please, please be there," she muttered to herself. It was only a few hundred feet, and they were there. By sheer desperation, she managed to open the gate. These horses were docile and so used to the inexperienced dudes who rode them that she had no trouble getting one by the mane. Getting up on its back, however, was quite another challenge, but she managed to coax it near the fence, using rails to struggle up onto its back. By now, darkness was fairly complete. The hospital-gowned, bareback rider and horse went through the ajar gate, across the yard and into the stand of aspens near the lodge.

The horse was reluctant to leave his equine friends but must have sensed her urgency. She laid her hands along the sides of his neck, kicked, and coaxed, and he made his way through the loose stand of aspens. When she thought she had cleared enough distance and it was dark enough, she aimed him in the general direction where she felt would be the highway. By now, she had a margin of safety, and her thoughts tried to make some sense out of what she had just experienced. Were they trying to kill her and these other people? No, she thought, probably not. She was very aware that her body was thinner. She tried and tried to recall the events of whatever the previous time period might have been. She remembered coming, meeting the people, going on the nature walk, the horseback ride, sitting down with Carl, the psychologist. That was it... That was her last recollection. From the point of the hypnotism session, something bad had happened to her, and whatever it was, she ended up strapped to a bed with an IV full of sedatives in her arm. The thought was horrifying. She pushed the horse to go faster. As he trotted, she again became aware of pain where she had pulled out that fully inflated bladder catheter.

CHAPTER 6

Amy's original intent had been to reach the highway on the horse and summon help, but as her mind retraced what she concluded must be going on, it occurred to her that if the entire fat farm and the community was a conspiracy of malevolence, some locals or even the local police might somehow be involved. She kept trying to convince herself that she was conjuring up additional paranoia but could not free her mind of the horrible thought that anyone who picked her up might be as likely to take her to an undesirable fate as to a good one. She decided that she would be careful. She turned the horse parallel to the highway, really not able to see much detail. She knew she would soon be very cold, but at least the horse below her was warm. Some houses along the highway, mostly cabins or small farmsteads, became visible as she approached them.

At first she believed she had some time on her hands, but then she remembered not closing the gate where the horses were held. If they were loose grazing around the yard, people at Rocky Mountain Restoration would begin seeking an explanation. The first house she came to was obviously occupied. A dog was barking and lights were on inside. She elected to ride past that. The second one was dark, a small frame-style house with a few corrals and a barn behind. There was a freestanding garage that would hold a single vehicle. The overhead door was open and the garage was empty. She rode up to the back of the house, slipped off her horse, and peered in a window. No sign of life. She tried the door. It was locked. She felt above the door jam. The key was there. On a different day, she would have felt rather smug for finding the key; however, there was no time for any editorializing thoughts, and she mechanically opened the door and went in. The telephone was easy to find. She only hesitated momentarily and dialed Pam.

After what seemed the longest two rings her sister answered. "Pam, it's Amy."

"Oh, hi, Amy. I just drove up to see you Friday, but you were out rafting on the Snake River, and they said you wouldn't be back for three days. Are you back already?"

Amy gasped. "Pam, I wasn't gone. I'm in a lot of trouble. I need you to come get me."

"What sort of trouble?" Pam asked.

"I can't explain now, but you need to come right now and get me."

"Okay, okay," Pam responded. "But it will take me two hours to get there, you know."

"Yes, I know," said Amy.

Pam sensed the urgency in her voice. "Where shall I meet you? In front of the lodge?"

"No, no, no," said Amy. "Look for me along the highway. I think I am..." She hesitated. "...south. I'm south on the highway, south of the lodge. Maybe a mile, maybe two." Her mind raced, how could she arrange this? "Leave your right turn blinker on all the time, so I know it's you. I will step up onto the roadway."

Pam said, "Amy, are you crazy? What is the matter?" Amy begged, "Trust me, just come now."

"Okay, I am leaving right now."

Thank heavens it was her sister she was dealing with here. Anyone else could probably not have responded without more explanation, but a sibling could understand.

"Pam, don't stop, don't talk to anyone until you find me." She hung up the phone, slipped through the house to a bedroom, rummaged around in a closet and found clothes. She thought, I need to take some from the back of a drawer or somewhere where they won't be missed too soon. She located a pair of jeans, too big, but they covered her; a jacket; socks; and some women's winter boots. She slipped out of the house as quickly as possible. The horse was gone as she expected. She walked a little bit away from the driveway then toward the highway.

She found a place to crouch down in some bushes along the barrow pit where she could see the roadway and waited.

Still terrified, Amy tried to organize her thoughts. Thankfully, the clothing she had procured was sufficient to stop the shivering. As she warmed, she became aware that her knee stung from being dragged along the cement. She tried to make conclusions out of the sensory impressions she had during her escape but realized there was not much information there. She recalled being in the small room and was certain that she had an IV in her arm, so she assumed she must have been drugged. All of her recollections of those few minutes or whatever time it might have been, however, were dreamlike and for a moment, she questioned their reality. Could she have simply had a bad dream and reacted so violently? Had she become mentally ill? She knew, however, that she had a sense of something sinister and had trusted her instincts thus far, so she determined to continue to carry out her plan.

She considered the humiliation she would experience had this, in fact, been a contrivance of her own mind. Thankfully, it was Pamela that was coming to pick her up.

She again set her mind to make sense of what had happened and planned what she might do next. She struggled again with the idea that she had overreacted to some trivial stimulation.

A police car sped by on the road, followed by a gray pickup truck with a police light bar and a sheriff's emblem. Amy was far enough in the barrow pit and well enough shielded by weeds that she was not much concerned about detection at this moment. However, two police vehicles going by at the same time caught her attention and curiosity, so she eased up nearer the roadway to a better vantage point to see where they might have turned. She could not entirely see the roadway to the center but had a general idea which direction and how far it might lie. An oncoming pair of headlights shooed her back down into the security of the roadside bushes. She reached back and tucked her long, light-colored hair into the jacket she was wearing, thinking that it might stand out and reflect the light, giving her position away. After the car passed, she slipped back toward the roadway. She could see headlights going away from the main highway eastward in the general vicinity of the lodge, she thought. She could also see behind the tongue of the hill, a substantial glow of light from the area where the lodge might have been. She wondered if there were always this many outdoor lights on or if this had something to do with her absence.

By now, a firm determination to complete her intended plan was well seated, and she settled back to watch for Pam. She studied each oncoming car carefully. In the darkness, it was difficult to make out colors, but she knew she was looking for a small, blue sedan. She hoped Pam would please remember to have her blinker on as instructed.

Blinking yellow lights caught her attention at almost that moment, but she recognized them as the amber lights of the police bar on the sheriff's pickup, which now came back the other way, this time with lights illuminated and traveling at a considerably higher rate of speed. Her natural assumption was to think they were looking for her, but she tried to convince herself otherwise.

The pickup did not travel far past her when it slowed, signaled for a turn and pulled into the farmhouse she had just burglarized. A panicky sensation came over her, and she suspected a connection would be made between the burglary and her departure from the center. She thought there likely were horse hoof prints in the yard, but since it was completely dark, she wondered if they would be discovered. Her mind raced through her image of a police investigation formed primarily from cop shows on TV, and she wondered if they would be dusting for fingerprints. She thought, I should have wiped off the telephone and been careful what I touched.

It then crossed her mind that she was no career criminal and shouldn't need to be concerned about these things. However, technically, she had just committed a burglary. Her inclination was to sneak along the roadway northward away from the farmhouse. That, however, would bring her closer to the lane to the restoration center where she surmised there might be considerable traffic as well. She settled the quandary by deciding to stay put. She wondered if she would be arrested and prosecuted, and now Pam would come looking for her and be implicated as an accomplice. Surely she could avoid any trouble for Pam and could explain her sister's innocence. She wondered if she could do jail time for petty burglary.

These thoughts stopped short when she mused, "Hey, I am the victim of a conspiracy or some other abusive act, and here I am worrying about being prosecuted myself. Get a grip on yourself,

Amy." Again, the doubts crept in. Perhaps she had been truly sick or injured, and they had to take care of her, and she had simply fled in a delusional state. She was, in fact, very stiff and weak still, and had been tremendously so when she first struggled out of the place. If that was true, though, why was she not in a hospital? Why were there dimly lit corridors made of concrete and so cold? And why were there other bodies in the same repose?

Time passed slowly, and she became impatient. There was not much traffic on the highway now. One pair of headlights approached a little more slowly than most of the others. Amy felt she should slink down in the brush a bit further because they might be looking for her. She estimated it had only been an hour and a half since she called Pam. She guessed she had about thirty more minutes to wait.

But no, there it was, the right blinker was on as the car moved slowly down the road. She wiggled up in the brush a little closer to the pavement and strained with all her effort to make out the color and shape of the car. As it approached, it was clearly not a police vehicle, and she recognized its general shape and was quite certain it was blue. Her pent-up anxiety propelling her, she burst up onto the roadway waving her arms. The car swerved to the right and came to an abrupt stop, skidding in the gravel as its right wheels left the shoulder of the road. Amy ran to the passenger side and pulled open the door with great relief.

Pam said, "Amy, you look terrible!"

"Turn your blinker off and start driving. I will explain as we go."

She slid down in the passenger seat and closed the door, and Pam began to drive. About a half a mile up the road, Amy could not resist peering up out of the seat a little bit to look across the dashboard to the farmhouse. Two gray sheriff's pickup trucks were parked there. All the lights were on in the house, and through the open draperies in the living room, she could see several people moving about. She quickly slunk back down in the vehicle. At first, she was inclined to point this out to Pam but thought Pam might slow the vehicle or respond in such a way that they would be detected, so she let her drive on by.

By now, Pam had a thousand questions. Amy tried to calm her excitement and began to explain the whole sequence of events as she could remember them. Pam interrupted, "By the way, where are we going?" It occurred to Amy that they should attempt a route of travel that would be not very conspicuous. It also occurred to her that they might eventually search for her at Pam's, but it would look more suspicious if Pamela were gone, so she determined they would go there for now. They took the first available secondary road and began detouring on an indirect route toward Pam's house.

CHAPTER 7

"Where's Brad?" inquired Amy, referring to Pam's six-year-old.

"Oh, he's home with Roger," she said. "Does Roger know where you went?"

"No, I think he knew something was up, though, because I left so fast."

"You certainly must have," Amy said. "It didn't seem like it took you long to get here."

"Well, it shouldn't have, as fast as I drove."

"Well, don't drive fast now. We can't afford to be picked up by the police."

Pam said again, "Amy, you look terrible. You're pale, thin, and frankly, you don't smell so good."

By now, Amy had recounted the events as she could recall them to Pamela and had sought feedback from her as to whether she might be delusional and paranoid or not. The family, however, had not been notified of any illness or sickness, and since Amy was unmarried, her immediate family was her next of kin.

Pam recited the events of the day of her visit to the center. She had come there looking for Amy, been greeted by Cindy, whom she had thought was most delightful and personable. Cindy had informed her of Amy's excellent weight-loss progress and fitness improvement and had shown her Amy's file. "I saw pictures of you riding horseback, playing volleyball, swimming in the pool, and sitting around a campfire with some other people," she said incredulously.

"Pam, the only recollection of any of those that I have is horseback riding."

"Well, get in my purse. They gave me a picture of you and some people playing volleyball. I think it is still in there." She flicked on the dome light in the vehicle, and Amy rummaged through the purse, shortly producing in her hand a snapshot of some people playing volleyball. Pam pointed. "See, that's you right there. That's even the same old grungy sweatshirt you always wear." Amy's eyes strained in the dim light. Yes, it was the same old grungy sweatshirt and it sure enough looked like her, but her face was mostly turned away from the camera.

"Who are the other people in the picture?" Pam inquired.

Amy studied the photo. "I don't know any of them that I can recognize." Well, wait a minute; the two joggers that she had seen when she first entered the center were there. She remembered them clearly.

"I think it isn't me," she said.

"Of course it's you. Who else in the world would have a sweatshirt like that?"

"Oh, it might be my sweatshirt, but I don't think it's me in it. Do I look like this from the back?"

"Well, I suppose about like that. I don't know, Amy. This whole thing is pretty weird," Pam said as she smiled and reached across to put her hand on her sister's shoulder. They leaned their heads together and drove on silently.

The garage door closed automatically behind them as they entered the house through the side door. Roger's mouth dropped when he saw Amy.

"My gosh," he exclaimed. "What happened to you?"

Pam was also astonished when she got a look at her sister in better light.

Roger said, "Someone from the police department called to see if Amy was here or if we knew anything about her. I thought you had gone to a PTA meeting. What's going on here?" Both Amy and Pam were grateful Roger had not known the truth.

"Where's Brad?" Pam said.

"He's sleeping," replied Roger, so Amy began again to recite her tale. Her eyes looked over to the kitchen counter top and a half-eaten plate of cookies. Instantly, the sensation of hunger overwhelmed her. Her eyes shot to the refrigerator with a level of desire similar to a drowning person's desire for air. She yanked open the refrigerator door, grabbed a carton of milk, and made for the cookies, almost not in control of herself. Roger and Pam watched with mouths agape as Amy embarked on this predator and prey relationship with cookies and milk. She wolfed the cookies down and was drinking milk straight from the carton, when she looked up, a white trickle coming out of the corner of her mouth, and realized how she must appear and what she was doing.

"Oh my," she mumbled through a mouthful of crumbs. "I must be starving." The realization hit them at all the same time. She was starving.

Roger cautioned not to overeat, and Pam helped her into the bathroom where a soak in a warm tub felt unbelievably good. A fresh pair of clothes and some more food later, Amy began to feel considerably better. The three of them sat down around the kitchen table to decide what to do.

◆

CHAPTER 8

Sheriff Hansen looked across his desk at his deputy. "Okay, we've got a missing-person report and a burglary in the same general vicinity. What was taken?" he said, rubbing his eyes, for by now it was late. "Just a pair of women's boots, as far as we know. Black."

"No sign of forced entry, right?"

"Right. The Howells just noticed their door was unlocked when they came home. They checked around and a pair of the missus's boots were gone."

"Okay, Tim, let me get this straight. Somebody who is buck naked, walks into somebody's house, takes a pair of boots, and walks out."

"That's what we know, Mike," he responded.

The sheriff mustered a half-hearted grin. "So what we are looking for is a woman in her early thirties, stark naked except for boots, right? Should be pretty easy to find. She's probably collected a crowd by now," he said with as much sarcasm as he could muster at midnight. "Okay, let's put this together," he went on. "First of all, how does Doc Fisher know she would have been naked in the first place? If he does know that, why does he know it? Second, how many naked people ride horses? So if the gate's open, did the horses just get out, or did she let them out? Third, if she only took boots from one place, and she was looking for clothes, she had to get them someplace else or she is dead of hypothermia by now."

"Mike, it is summer, more or less. It is not that cold."

"It's forty degrees or colder," the sheriff responded. "I don't know many naked people who can survive a night at forty degrees. So she is either in real trouble, or she has found a place to hole up or been picked up hitchhiking or whatever. There's not much traffic this time of night, and since there are only two ways out of this valley on pavement, let's put a deputy at either end and stop cars for the next few hours. We better get the search-and-rescue boys out and do a flashlight search of the area around the fat farm. If she is in the woods around there, she won't have long to survive, and if she is as crazy as it looks like she is, she won't be making any good decisions whether she has gotten cold or not."

"Mike, do you think you are overreacting a little to put road blocks at either end of the valley for somebody who stole property totaling less than fifty bucks?"

"Yeah, we're gonna to do it," he said, stretching his hands behind his head. "I know it is not much, but I haven't seen Doc Fisher this revved up in a long time. His place brings a lot of money into our little valley, and we need it. The last thing they want over there is a bunch of bad publicity. He is a good guy, running a decent business, and we will settle this thing quickly and quietly for him. You get on it, and I will notify the state boys in case they see a suspicious vehicle out of county." His hand reached for the telephone as he spoke. Twenty minutes later, Deputy Tim was standing in front of a disheveled midnight crew of volunteer search-and-rescue people at the fire station.

"Okay, we want a grid-type search of the area around the fat farm for about a thousand yards on either side, or as far as you can get up the slope on the east."

He went on, "They say over there, this woman has gone berserk and run out of there, more or less bare, so she could be hypothermic by now. We need to have some warming gear with us. She might have rounded up some clothes. Be cautious. We don't think she is particularly dangerous, but she has got to be off her cork some to do this, so be a little careful. Now let's get this done and get her found and get back home." He stepped down off the running board of the fire truck, walked over, got into his own pickup, and led a small parade of headlights north of town toward the Rocky Mountain Center.

Cindy hung up the phone receiver and said, "They are sending out a search-and-rescue squad to look the area over."

"Let's hope they find her," replied Dr. Fisher. "If she stays missing or gets away things could get complicated. Frankly, it would be simpler to explain away a death."

"Oh, we'll find her." Cindy grimaced. "She doesn't have that many places to go, so if she is not out there shivering to death now, she's just got the one sister and her folks and the place she works. No steady boyfriend, one girlfriend she sent a post card to after she got here, and some acquaintances in the apartments where she lives. Lawrence felt like he got a really good handle on her during the horse ride."

"Well, we better solve this fast because we have got a new bunch coming in only a few days."

"I know," said Cindy, "all the knowledgeable staff are out driving around looking already, and Lawrence found the horse an hour ago, not a quarter mile from the corrals."

"Are the rest of the horses all accounted for?"

"Yes," replied Cindy.

"Do the cops know we found her horse?"

"No, we haven't told them yet."

"Well, we better notify them, or it will look funny. How are you so sure she escaped on the horse, anyway?" "Blood on the corral gate about knee high and no bleeding horses that we know about. Besides, the blood was on the outside of the gate according to Lawrence." "Okay, as long as we have got our story straight, let's go on. Did you check the tape on the IVs on everybody else?"

"Yes, checked and double checked."

"All right, is the false door properly installed, because we're going to have a lot of people snooping around here for a few days?"

"Uh huh. Don't you think we should just let people up now and discharge them a few days early?"

"No, it will cause suspicion. We should stay with the plan-find Amy. Carl will do the mental health evaluation, and she will be in a loony bin faster than she can blink. He'll have her so full of thorazine she will have no credibility."

"I sure hope you're right," Cindy said.

"People have psychotic breakdowns all the time. She is the perfect age, and she is enough of a loner that this will be easy. All we have to do is locate her," he said.

"All right," she responded curtly. "I still think you are pressing your luck lowering the temperature like that." "Listen, the calorie consumption at those lower temperatures is phenomenal. We can shorten our turnaround time so dramatically that we can easily raise revenues twenty percent without affecting our overhead in the least. I know you are panicky, but we didn't have a death here, we had an escapee. The problem wasn't the temperature. The problem was a tape deficiency on the IV, and that," he growled, "is your department."

Cindy turned her face away as he finished this remark. "Cindy, I'm sorry. You are the best. It is a simple mistake, and I am confident it won't happen to you again. We just need to solve this problem. If we can stay in business a few more years, we are done, set for life, out of here. No risks, no questions. I will retire, write a couple of books on weight loss. A piece of cake. We just have to find her quickly, that's all," he said sternly. "I am worried one of the knowledgeables will squeal," she said.

"I don't think so; they will be implicated if they do, and those fat pension plans they are anticipating will disappear. Human nature is a powerful thing. The only squealers will be unknowledgeable staff or bystanders. Why don't you get some sleep? I'll go schmooze with the search-and-rescue boys and see you in the morning." He stood up, grabbed a jacket, and walked out the office door.

CHAPTER 9

A dozen or so search-and-rescue volunteers combed the area around the lodge with flashlights. Since this was a rural area, one search dog was available and with the group as well, a slender German shepherd named Chief. Chief scented Amy's presence in the hedgerow and chokecherry on the southeast corner of the lodge where Amy had come out.

About a half an hour after the search had begun, Sheriff Hansen's gray pickup truck rolled into the lane to Rocky Mountain Center and made its way up the gravel road. Dr. Fisher was standing on the deck outside with the collar of his jacket turned up against the evening chill. He could see Sheriff Hansen talking on the radio as he pulled in and parked. Sheriff Hansen stepped out of the pickup truck, replacing his wide brimmed hat.

"Any leads, Mike?" Dr. Fisher inquired.

"No, Doc, nothing yet, but the night's still young. We will leave deputies at either end of the valley checking cars till about sunup at least. We don't want to cause undue alarm over something like this by daytime checks, but until people start out for work in the morning, there won't be much traffic, and we can check it easily."

"Thanks, Mike, I appreciate your help. I am concerned she will get herself hurt or lost if we don't find her pretty soon. It has been a while since I did my psychiatric training in med school, but I know a bona fide psychotic breakdown when I see one," he continued.

Mike responded, "What do you say we go in and you tell me a little more about it, Doc."

"Sure, come on in. We'll sit in my office."

Sheriff Hansen slouched in the leather, overstuffed chair across from Dr. Fisher, who sat at his desk. The sheriff's main objective was to get enough information about Amy that he might have some idea where to look for her, and Dr. Fisher knew that. Neither man was suspicious of the other. However, Mike made mental note that the doctor's demeanor seemed agitated a little more than one might have expected for this, but he wrote it off as a businessman simply worried about bad publicity.

"Mike, we screen people so carefully before they come here. I interview them and do a physical exam on everyone after they arrive so as to avoid this kind of thing in the first place. There are a lot of cuckoos out there who think if they come to a place like ours, it will correct their messed-up lives. You know we have been very careful about whom we will accept. I guess Amy just fooled me on this one." He went on with an expressionless face, "People who have acute psychotic breakdowns often manifest some warning signs like being loners and socially withdrawn from their friends. This is particularly true of those who are destined to have schizophrenia, but some folks just undergo a psychotic breakdown and then get better. I suspect Amy will be one of those because we were unable to detect any warning signs in our evaluation. As I thought about it, though, she is sort of a loner. An attractive gal her age, no steady boyfriend. She told us she has one girlfriend that is kind of close, and that's about all we know."

Mike nodded enough that the doctor knew he was paying attention.

"I hope for Amy's sake that it is an acute psychotic event that she gets over. She seemed to be a nice enough lady otherwise. I still sort of kick myself for not figuring this out sooner. I saw a couple of cases like this in the valley when I first came here and was running my family practice." He shrugged. "I guess I've been away from general medicine too long since we opened this place, and maybe I got rusty. Carl had expressed concerns when he interviewed her as well, and I probably should have paid more attention to her psychological profile."

Sheriff Hansen let him finish and after a pause said, "That's water under the bridge, Doc. Now help me figure out what she is likely to behave like now."

"Well, it is unpredictable, Mike. Most psychotic people are paranoid, so they are afraid of things, but it is hard to say what they might be afraid of. The majority of them have delusional ideas like space aliens are trying to get them or it's their health care providers or the neighbors or about anybody. That's why if you all find her, you need to be a little careful picking her up. She is likely to have some sort of delusions of somebody or something out to get her. Can you imagine, Mike, having a condition that puts ideas like that in your head?

It must be horrible for those folks. Thank God we have some medications that help them at least somewhat."

The doctor leaned forward a little. "You remember the Waterses' boy, don't you? His folks ran that Hereford operation down the valley here. A and B student until he was a junior in high school, then just dropped out of sight for about a year, and the next time I saw him, he was absolutely certain that space travelers were using his dad's cattle to get messages to earth. He has been in and out of institutions since, and I think they have him in the state hospital again right now. The darn kid quits taking his medications and relapses."

The sheriff nodded in understanding, having been called to the Waterses' home on several occasions to maintain the peace.

The doctor continued, "At any rate, if we find Amy and she is in that state, I think we can still do an involuntary seventy-two-hour commitment for an evaluation, can't we?"

The sheriff again nodded in affirmative.

"Do you still need an MD signature on those, Mike? Or would it be better to have Carl commit her to the seventy-two hours?"

Mike responded that an MD signature would probably carry more weight, but he was sure the judge would go along with it in any event, since it was pretty standard procedure.

Mike found himself feeling pretty tired. Lounging in the chair in the wee hours of the morning didn't help any, and he stood to stretch a little. "Doc, do you suppose I could just look around a little bit? I guess technically I ought to have a warrant, and I could get one if you want me to."

"Of course you don't need a warrant, Mike. Look around all you want. I will go with you if you like. We have gathered up most of her belongings, if they would be of any use to you in your investigation."

Mike responded that they might be useful at a later time, but he wasn't too concerned about them now. He had made a point not to mention the burglary of a pair of boots down the road, which he expected was associated with Amy. Dr. Fisher may have been aware of it already, but as long as the doctor didn't mention it, neither would he. They could probably use her luggage to obtain fingerprints if they got to that point in this thing. At this time, he wasn't so much worried about prosecuting Amy as a criminal as just helping apprehend her and seeing that she got adequate treatment for whatever might be wrong. The story that Dr. Fisher recited seemed absolutely plausible. After a walk around the place with the doctor, he decided not to snoop any further for the time being without proper legal paperwork.

By now, the searchers were congregating back on the yard around the lodge, having turned up nothing. Sheriff Hansen spoke briefly to his deputy, and they dismissed the search team. Chief had only been able to follow the scent for a short distance over toward the corrals and then seemed unable to locate it anymore. Deputy Tim said there was some suspicion she had left on a horse, but that all the horses had been found and were accounted for-one, however, having been found somewhat later.

The deputy said, "Mike, it's been a pretty long night, and you may have to face the public in the morning. Go catch a couple hours sleep. I will check with the guys down on the highways, and I am going to drive by that farm again and look for hoof prints. Talk to you in a couple of hours."

Sheriff Hansen nodded and climbed in his truck.

CHAPTER 10

Amy looked firmly at her brother-in-law. "Roger, it has to be malicious. It wasn't just me. I saw those others, including Dave, in cubicles with IVs in the dark."

Pam chimed in, "How else can you explain it?"

"Well, it's hard to argue with what you saw unless you were delirious or something," he countered. "Look at how skinny you are so fast. Maybe you were sick or dieted too hard, and it affected your mind."

"I don't think so." Amy said. "I know how Cindy was talking. I'm sure I didn't imagine that. And someone else was in my cabin!"

"Amy, don't get me wrong. You know I'm always on your side. We just better be sure what's real before you react to it."

Pam injected, "We should call Mom and Dad."

"I'm not so sure," Roger contended. "If your folks don't even know you're missing, we don't need to tell them you're found. This forces the other side to play their hand a little bit. And if somebody contacts your parents, we will be the first to know about it, and we can reassure them then."

Amy said, "You are always so logical, but that does make sense."

He was already jotting down notes. "Two things trouble me. One is their motivation. The other is how could all those people know nothing of what happened to them? Unless it's some government experiment or something. Whatever, if it's all true then it's a big deal."

CHAPTER 11

After a few fitful hours of sleep, all were up and about at Pam's house. Roger headed off to work at the Federal Engineering Laboratory, where he was employed as a supplies and procurement manager. Pam had decided to have things look like business as usual around their home. By about seven a.m., Amy called her friend, Sue Barnes.

"Hi, Sue. It's Amy. Are you awake?"

"Yeah, more or less," a sleepy voice responded. "Are you having any fun up there?"

"No, not really. That's why I am calling," Amy returned.

While not her closest friend, Sue and Amy spent every day together in the same cubicle and knew each other well, including, at least on a reasonably detailed level, each other's hopes, fears, attitudes, men problems, and so on. She felt comfortable getting right to the point.

"Sue, when you were at the Rocky Mountain Center, did anything strange happen to you?"

"What do you mean, strange?"

"Well, did they give you any drugs or did you have any weird dreams or strange experiences with hypnotism?" "Well, no, I wouldn't say strange. You know they had that psychologist give you some suggestions to help you lose weight," she said. "I didn't see any harm in that."

"Well, I think they were doing weird stuff to me," Amy responded. "I woke up in a dark, cement room that was cold and I had an IV in my arm."

"For weird!" the voice on the other end of the phone responded. "Did you ask them why?"

"Actually, no, I just snuck out of there," she said. "I think they are probably looking for me."

"So call them and see what the deal is. Maybe you were sick. If you lose weight fast, a lot of people get sick."

"No, Sue, I think there is something illegal going on there," she continued.

Sue was a little more awake now. "Well, are you okay now?"

"Yeah, I think I am okay now."

"Well, where are you?" Sue inquired.

"I think I would rather not say. It is probably better if you don't know."

"Amy, you are being pretty strange. Are you sober?" she said in an accusing tone.

"Yeah, I'm sober," she said. "Listen, you need to get to work, and I am fine, so do me a favor and don't say anything to anybody at work. I will try to call you tonight. Will you be home?"

"I've got a date at seven, but I will be home till then." Normally, Amy would have inquired about the date, but today, she had weightier matters on her mind. "Okay Sue, keep quiet about this, all right?"

"Sure."

Amy laid the receiver down gently and stared thoughtfully into space for a few minutes.

Pam brought her back to earth. "Well, what did she say?"

"She doesn't believe me. She thinks I am drunk or I was on something."

"Surely Sue knows that wouldn't be like you?"

"Well, I suppose it does sound pretty weird. The trouble is, I don't know what to do now. I guess I could turn myself in for taking the clothes. As far as I know, I wouldn't be in trouble for anything else, and the police could straighten the whole thing out." She paused. "That is, as far as I know, but I don't know what I have been doing for the last nineteen days."

It had occurred to her last night that she didn't know what day it was, so when Pam told her, she had counted backwards on the calendar to the day she had arrived at the center. Since she only had recollection of those first three days there, she had a nineteen-day hole in her memory. She had also weighed herself, 112 pounds, too skinny for even her petite frame. Her body knew it too. Even though it kind of upset her stomach, she just couldn't eat enough toast and jelly that morning.

The two women spent a little time planning their next move, either to pursue the conspiracy idea somehow and involve law enforcement, or simply for Amy to go home and forget the whole thing. She knew there would be repercussions at her firm, however, they having paid for her stay there. Also, her car and a few important belongings were still at the lodge. She wished Sue had been more helpful. By about ten, Amy was still eating, and the two of them had decided to wait until Roger got home. He had promised to take off early in the afternoon if he could. About then, Pam reminded Amy that she had a home answering machine from which she could retrieve messages from another phone. Amy determined to check messages at her apartment. It took a few tries but then the spiel of messages, almost a month's worth, began. There was the usual series of messages, somebody wants this and somebody wants to sell her something or remind her to confirm her dental appointment. There was one message from a guy named Ben she had met at a friend's birthday party. He was interested in getting together for dinner.

Amy opened her eyes wider and gestured to the receiver with her finger, however, as one message exclaimed, "This is the Lincoln County Sheriff's Department. We have been asked to open a missing person's case, and you are the missing person. If you are home or come home, will you please call us so that we can close this investigation?" The dispatcher's voice then went on to give the particulars of phone number and so on and the name of Sheriff Mike Hansen. The next message was the voice of Bill O'Hara.

"Amy, Bill O'Hara calling." It went on, "Sue talked to me this morning."

Amy felt a small wave of anger bring blood to her face.

The voice went on, "She said she wouldn't have spoken to me except that someone called the office this morning looking for you and wouldn't give their name. So she asked me if I had been called too. I haven't, and I don't suppose anything is out of order at Rocky Mountain. I just hope you are okay and thought you ought to know." A mechanical voice then came on the line saying, "End of messages," and then automatically hung up the phone with a click.

Amy looked over at her sister. "The plot thickens, Pammie. Have you got anything else to eat?"

CHAPTER 12

Amy's palms were sweaty as she picked up the phone to call. She had, after talking it over with Pam, felt guilty enough to have somebody's sheriff department looking for her, that she wanted to let them know she was all right and not to worry. She, furthermore, thought it would probably be wise to have them on her side. She could return the borrowed clothes and boots and hoped that they would go easy on her when they heard her circumstances. She knew she had easy access to legal assistance if she needed it. She had toyed with calling one of the attorneys before calling the sheriff's department but knew that she would have the right to obtain an attorney in plenty of time anyway, having a certain familiarity with the ins and outs of the justice system.

The voice on the other end of the phone answered the ringing, "Lincoln County Sheriff's Department." "Yes, may I speak with Sheriff Hansen, please?" "May I say who is calling?"

"I am returning his call. I would rather identify myself to him directly, please."

A short pause on the other end of the line, and then the answer, "Okay, I will transfer the call."

Amy thought, Thank heavens it is a small town sheriff's department, not too much red tape.

Sheriff Hansen was quickly identifying himself on the other end of the line. Amy's voice trembled slightly, although she wasn't sure why. "Sheriff Hansen, this is Amy Crockett. I think you might have been looking for me."

He didn't miss a beat. "Why, yes we have, Amy. The people at Rocky Mountain Restoration had asked us to open a missing person's case on you, since you seem to be lost." He paused briefly, leaving the conversation open ended, hoping she might volunteer information useful to him. He had enough experience in law enforcement to know not to monopolize the conversation and allow his suspects to betray themselves by their words. She didn't take the bait, however, and so he continued, "The first thing I am interested in is whether you are okay or not."

This time she answered, "Yeah, I am okay I think." "Where are you?" came his quick reply.

She was ready for this one. "I'd rather not say till I know what's going on."

She could almost hear him smile on the other end of the phone. He had expected that one and was ready.

"Well then, Amy, I will try to tell you what's going on. First, there is no official missing-person's case here because for adults, you have to be missing for seventy two hours before we can formally open a case. We have, however, been looking for you and have been concerned for your welfare. Unless I can make some sort of positive identification of you within that seventy-two-hour frame work, we will still have to open the case and have people hunting all over heck for you." He figured this might reel her in.

She was sharper than he had guessed though.

"Well, is it against the law to be missing?" she said.

"No, not exactly, Amy, but it still makes a lot of work for us, and unless you want to spend a lot of effort hiding, somebody from law enforcement is going to have to go to the trouble to find you and identify you." Again a pause... Again, no response.

"Amy, there is also the matter that you are a suspect in a burglary here in our town. We will be needing to get that issue dealt with." She didn't seem like much of a criminal to him and he had already done her computerized background check and found nothing, so he quickly continued, "Of course, you are presumed innocent in this case, but we still need to settle the matter. If you would be kind enough to give me your whereabouts, we can take the necessary steps to solve this."

Sheriff Hansen still wasn't sure whether he was dealing with a sane person or not based on Dr. Fisher's discourse the night before, although she seemed pretty sane so far. She seemed even more sane to him when she responded.

"Okay," she said with as much self-confidence as she could muster. "I would like to make a deal with you. I can save you from your missing-person's paperwork and maybe even try to help with your burglary case, if you like, if you will handle things my way."

Ooh, he had a sharp one on his hands here! She had set him up and tempted him without admitting any guilt. He wondered how someone in a full-blown psychosis could reason this well.

"What way would you like to handle this, Amy?"

"I'd like to get together with you on neutral ground," she said. "All I am asking is that you hear my story out completely before you do anything else—and that includes talking to anyone else, even in your department. If you will do that, I will cooperate with you in any way I can." She was surprised at herself for giving in so easily, but even over the telephone, something about the sheriff made her feel like he was one of the few up there she could trust. She knew she might be wrong, but she was trusting her feelings as much as her head.

On the other end of the phone line, the sheriff was doing the same. Professionally he knew he should remain skeptical, but agreed to her terms since no other simple alternative offered itself.

Amy assertively went on, "I will call you with a time and place to meet tomorrow." And before she chickened out, she hung up the phone.

Mike sat back in his chair, half-smiling, hands behind his head. He was pretty good at judging people's character. He figured this one was no criminal, and she didn't seem out of her mind. He prided himself on being flexible enough to get the job done. He figured it was human nature that if he extended her some trust, she might extend him some.

The smile faded a little, though, as he thought he might have just been out bargained by a suspect. He had no reason to suspect her to be violent, and was sure he could handle the situation in a safe manner depending on where she chose to meet him.

What Amy didn't know was he was already prepared to negotiate with her. The more he considered what he had seen and what he had heard from the people at the fat farm, the more the incongruity bothered him. Granted, when he had walked through last night with Dr. Fisher, everything seemed fine enough, but it troubled him that a couple of things seemed out of place. Specifically, the whole campus was kind of in an uproar with search-and-rescue people around the area, a search dog, police cars coming in and out, and lights on all over, yet none of the clients were out wandering around the place to see what was going on. From the number of cars in the parking lot, there should have been enough people around there that some of them would be up wandering around in their robes voyeuristically watching the happenings.

Every cop knows that people love to gawk, he thought. He wondered if Amy could shed some light on this oddity.

Being a man of his word, he stood from his desk, donned his brimmed hat, avoided his secretary's questioning eyes on the way out, saying "I'll be in the patrol car for a while," and went through the door.

CHAPTER 13

The sheriff drove leisurely the length of the valley and back, paying particular attention to look up toward the Rocky Mountain Center when he passed it going each way. His mind was trying to put together what his five senses had told him about the situation. He was also trying to decide what his sixth sense was telling him to do. He was a man who trusted his instincts and his judgment of other people. It had almost gotten him in trouble a couple of times, like when he was faced with a shotgun-armed, drunk, and depressed fellow a few years ago.

The man was coming unglued because of family problems and was threatening everybody around him, as well as himself, with a shotgun. Since such responsibility rested with the sheriff in this county, Mike had to go in and try to do something about it. He tried to talk the fellow down and managed to get everybody else out of the house. He thought he had him defused pretty well, but he was holed up in the back bedroom, so Mike yelled, "I am coming out into view now, Ed, put the gun down!" but as he rounded the corner, he found himself looking right down the barrel of the shotgun about a dozen feet away across the tiny bedroom. Police protocol would have recommended that Mike drop to one side and fire his weapon in this circumstance, but he had known Ed for eight years, so he played by his guts rather than by the book. Ed himself had hesitated, too, which allowed Mike to close the twelve feet between them. What ended up was a wrestling match over the shotgun. Mike still had a place on his scalp where the hair grew a little uneven from the laceration he had sustained, but he had managed to wrest the gun free and get Ed sobered up and straightened out.

He hated these social and family crisis situations. That was not why he had gone into law enforcement, but every time he drove past the auto body shop where the man worked, Ed would give him a two fingered salute, sort of a wave. Mike would think how satisfied he felt having not put a bullet in the man.

A low-slung red car with California plates heading away from Jackson Hole passed him in the opposite lane. Mike could see with the naked eye that the car was far in excess of the speed limit, but he had his radar gun off. He was driving to think. He would let the speeders roll by a few more hours and catch some of those guys later. One nice thing about small-town law enforcement was that the serious stuff tended to come one thing at a time.

He picked up his radio and talked to his dispatcher measuring his words carefully, since he knew that in the slow-paced rural life, many citizens listened to police scanners for entertainment. The dispatcher told him that among a few other phone calls, some unidentified caller said he would know who it was and she would try back. He responded that he would be in shortly to take care of those matters and drove toward town. He stopped in at the office long enough to tell the dispatcher to give the unidentified female caller his cell phone number if she called again, and he made a point to do this in person so it wasn't heard over the scanners and said he would take care of the other matters. He then called the deputy on duty, checked out, and headed home. The girls in the sheriff's office smiled knowingly to each other as he walked out the door, and once it had closed behind him, the chatter began-an unidentified female caller with Sheriff Hansen giving out his personal phone number. It made for good small-town gossip, and, anyway, most of the women around the department just didn't feel right about having a good catch like Mike unattached for so long. The department staff speculated about this over their work and by evening, rumors of the sheriff's new romance, in their embellished form, were circulating.

Mike pulled into his driveway, got out of the truck, patted his English setter's head, and entered from the back door. It was a tidy frame house with clean lines, a small shed and some corrals behind. Its porch wrapped around, complete with a swing and shuttered windows. It had once been the headquarters for a moderately prosperous family farm, but the land had been sold and the Millers had moved to Arizona to spend their retirement. Mike had rented the place for a couple of years, and although Mr. Miller had kept giving him the option to buy, he was just not feeling particularly permanent in the place. The house was certainly suitable but would have benefited considerably from some spiffing up, which he just hadn't had the interest to do, nor to spend the money to have it done. He tossed his gun and cartridge belt over onto the couch, set his hat on the kitchen table, leaned back in a dining room chair with his feet up on the table, and dialed the phone.

Dr. Fisher still sounded a bit agitated through his professed calmness to Mike as he said, "Any leads, Sheriff?"

"Not much, Doc. How about you all? Have you heard anything?"

"No, we have had no word here," he said.

The sheriff baited him slightly. "I thought maybe you had. A dispatcher said you called me three times today." "Well, I was interested in what was going on, of course. I took an oath to be concerned about my patients, or in this case clients, didn't I?"

"I know, Doc. I am only giving you a hard time," said the sheriff.

"Anyway, Mike, we are going to have a number of our clients back in here tomorrow. I didn't know if it would help you to interview them, but I thought I would let you know in case you wanted to. Several of Amy's group will be departing within the next couple of days."

Mike thought a minute. Maybe it would be useful to talk to a few of the folks. "So, Doc, when you say 'coming back in,' what do you mean?"

Doctor Fisher responded that many of their clients went to locations away from the lodge for several days at a time as part of their program. He indicated that several of the people would be coming back from a fishing trip in Yellowstone Park.

"Oh, I see. How does fishing in Yellowstone Park keep you from being fat, Doc?" he teased.

"Well, it does if you hike far enough to the river," responded the doctor sharply. "Mike, you know we try to teach these people healthy lifestyle choices so that when they leave our place they can continue to do things they enjoy to keep them healthier and in better shape."

"I know, Doctor," said the sheriff. "I am just joshing you a little. Don't you need a police escort on some of those back-country fishing trips? I could bring my own pole, and I know how to bait my own hook." He chuckled.

"Sure, Mike, we could take you along sometime. Why don't you just pay your fee, and we will enroll you in the whole program? We could have a guy like you in great shape in no time."

"Okay, Doc, you're on," he said. "Listen, I will let you know as soon as we have anything. We are working on several leads right now. I will drop by in the morning and interview your people, if that's all right."

Doctor Fisher seemed relieved at this remark, and the conversation ended.

Mike turned to his refrigerator and opened the door. It looked like the menu for tonight would be hot dogs and orange juice. He walked to the back screen door of his house and pushed it open. Max trotted in, tail wagging. Turning back toward the refrigerator door, he spied a carton of milk he had missed before. He spoke out loud to the dog, "It would be stupid to have hot dogs when you could have Sugar Puffs, wouldn't it, boy?" retrieving the milk as he spoke. The cereal clattered into the bowl. Max wagged his whole rear half expectantly by the table. Mike grinned down at him.

"I guess it does look like dog food. Ah, here, rot your teeth," and he set the first bowl down on the floor and poured a second one for himself.

With a few calories in their stomachs, man and dog felt the fatigue of being up most of the previous night settling about them, and both dozed on the couch in front of the gently droning television.

The ring of the phone brought him back alert, but Mike must have mumbled as he answered it. Amy's voice said, "Sheriff Hansen, is that you?" "Yes, it is," he replied. "This must be Amy." "Yes, it is. Do we still have an agreement?" She was very businesslike.

"Yes, I believe we do," he said.

"Good," she said, "then you won't be looking for me like a missing person and alarming my friends and family, will you?"

"A deal's a deal," he responded.

"Okay," she went on. "How about if we meet at that truck stop on Highway 89 just where you turn off to go to Jackson Hole at ten in the morning?"

"I think that would be fine. Do you need a way to get there? I can send an officer."

"No, I can arrange transportation," she said coyly. "All right, ten it is." He laid the phone down contentedly and man and dog were again lost in their dreams.

CHAPTER 14

By seven a.m., Sheriff Hansen's truck was parked in front of the lodge. Cindy was leading him along the path toward the bungalows. They stopped at the first one and tapped at the door.

"Are you up in there?" she inquired.

A man's voice responded, "Gettin' up. Come on in," and Dave pulled the door open, knees sticking out below his terry cloth bathrobe.

"Sorry to come by so early," said Cindy with her usual gregarious smile, which immediately calmed. "This is Sheriff Hansen," she went on. "He wants to ask a couple of questions about Amy, if that's all right."

"Sure, no problem," said Dave. Cindy turned abruptly and walked back down the path, leaving the two men looking at each other. "Come on in," said Dave. "I'm just getting up and around. So what's this about Amy?" he said. "Around here they are saying she had some sort of nervous breakdown and had to leave. At first I couldn't figure out why they were telling all of us that, but then I supposed they thought we would hear about it in town or somewhere. So why's the sheriff's department involved?" Mike responded that she had left her car and belongings, which made it an informal missing-person's evaluation and he just wondered if Dave had noticed anything about Amy that might be evidence of any instability or illness.

"Heck no," he responded. "I liked her. I was hoping I would get to spend more time around her. She must have been gone quite awhile because I don't think I've seen her since, well, two or three weeks ago." He looked puzzled as he spoke.

The sheriff seized the moment. "Well, that would seem funny that you wouldn't have seen her at all in that much time, being right here in the same program," he queried.

"Well, yeah, but I have been gone quite a bit. Been up to Yellowstone fishing. You ought to see this fish I caught." He started rummaging through the stack of papers and folders on the small rustic desk in the cabin producing a hand full of snapshots, which he rapidly thumbed through, proudly displaying one.

"Look at that, six and a half pounds," he said. Sure enough, there was a picture of Dave holding a big rainbow trout that looked every bit of six and a half pounds. The only thing bigger was the smile on Dave's face. The picture was taken in front of the lodge, however, and the sheriff said, "Where did you catch him?" "upper Snake River, above Jackson Lake," was the reply.

"Flies?"

"On flies, yeah."

"What kind of fly are they taking this time of year?" the sheriff persisted.

Dave hesitated, "Uhhh, you know I am not sure I can tell you exactly what we were using at the time." He seemed to recover his composure. About that time, Thomas strode through the door, seeming surprised to see a sheriff there. Introductions were made, and Mike explained his reason for inquiry. Thomas also responded he had noticed nothing out of the ordinary about Amy except that maybe Dave was kind of sweet on her and that usually meant trouble. He then turned to his buddy and remarked how glad he was that they had the laundry facility at the lodge since their clothes had smelled so much like fish. Mike asked a few more questions about their activities and then left.

By 9:30, he had pulled up to the truck stop at the Jackson turn off and backed his truck in the side parking area, tested his radio, and settled in to wait for Amy. He played a blind hunch that she would be coming from the Idaho side, and he was right. He recognized her from the photos at the center. She pulled up in a blue sedan with Idaho plates with another couple who must be her sister and brother-in-law. He had done his homework. He had two deputies on either side within two minutes by vehicle. They were not exactly privileged to know the goings on, but were on standby just in case. Mike had his radio mouthpiece attached to his shirt for easy access. Not that he was so worried about the confrontation; he just didn't want Amy slipping away.

Roger got out of the car, followed by Amy and then Pam, who had been driving. Roger strode over to the sheriff first, shook his hand, and introduced himself pointing out Amy and then his wife. The sheriff nodded, acknowledging in their direction.

The truck stop served as a tourist attraction. There were three outdoor tables with umbrellas over them. It was a warm June morning, and the four agreed to sit outside at a table and talk things over. Pam went in the café to buy sodas since no one was in the mood for anything else.

Mike was all business and on duty, but he had to admit that the well-defined lines of Amy's face were attractive and her personality just as he'd assessed it so far. She was well kept and scrubbed, with just enough makeup on that he couldn't be sure if she was wearing any. Her blond hair lay gently across her shoulders. She was thin but soft looking. There was a resemblance between the sisters, although Pam was darker with shorter-cropped hair and glasses. Everybody seemed hesitant to start at first, so the sheriff took charge, saying, "I appreciate you coming to meet me. I will hold up my end of the bargain and listen to what you have to say."

Amy began recitation of her tale describing her first days at the center. She then went on to relate her escape. The sheriff just sat back and listened.

"I'm sorry, Sheriff, but I'm not sure I was mentally clear when I first woke up, so my recollection is kind of dreamlike for the first few minutes."

Mike made a mental note that if Amy was trying to contrive this story for some reason, she had just damaged her credibility by admitting her memory of the events was impaired. He had considered whether she might be a disgruntled patron looking to cash in on a lawsuit. If so, she was not as smart as he judged her.

Maybe she was a drug user covering up. Maybe a publicity hound. Who knew? He needed to remind himself that one option was she was telling the truth – as far fetched as it sounded. And the major likelihood was she was crazy like the Doc said. But she sure didn't seem crazy.

"Mainly what I remember seeing was the little rooms with beds or cots and the IVs. After I pulled out that catheter tube thing, the pain really woke me up. That's when I noticed the headphones, I think. I mean when I opened the door, I could see better."

Roger interrupted. "I've got some theories about what's going on down there if you're interested. I've read about these kinds of experiments before."

"Thanks, Roger, but I'd like to let Amy finish first if that's okay. Amy, are you sure it was Cindy you heard?" "Uh huh. I know it was her. But the man could be anybody. I just couldn't tell."

She continued explaining how she had escaped and met Pam. "I brought back the boots and clothes I took from the house. Sorry, I was cold and didn't know what else to do."

"That's good," he said, not letting on that all they found missing was boots.

"I have some ideas about what could be happening if you'd like to hear them."

The sheriff was all ears. "Absolutely."

"See, I was having a dream I remember pretty well. But it was weird, about low-fat foods and grocery shopping. I think everybody has strange dreams, but this was an odd topic for me. Maybe because I was at that place and they talked about food and diets and things. But what if those headphones were for putting ideas in the people's minds, you know? The funny thing is, Pam got this picture of me and I don't remember anything about that day, but I kind of remember other things, only not really."

"What do you mean exactly?" Mike thought this was sounding more like nervous breakdown symptoms now. Probably the Doc was right about her.

"Well, I have this vague recollection of floating in a boat or raft, but I can't really recall where it was or how I got there or who else was there." She squinted as if trying to concentrate and inattentively pushed her hair back off her shoulders, her collarbones well defined under pale, smooth skin.

Pam produced the snapshot, pointing out it was Amy's clothes on whoever was in the picture.

"Amy, do you have an explanation?"

"Well, no, not exactly, and this all must sound crazy to you it sounds crazy to me, but that's how I remember it. Has anybody else had a situation like this?"

Mike felt he could answer without compromising. "No, this is the only complaint I've ever heard about the fa – uh, center." He worried "fat farm" might offend her.

It struck him that crazy people were not usually very willing to admit their craziness-yet Amy was most willing. His guts told him she was okay. Frankly, he liked her, but determined to remain objective.

Roger chimed in again that Amy had seemed perfectly normal to him and continued with his conviction that mind-altering experiments were being done and more or less that Mike should get to the bottom of it right away. With his inference that this must be CIA, FBI, or government subversives, he seemed more the crazed one than Amy.

Amy continued, "I lost over twenty pounds in nineteen days-but I never remember being hungry till I got away. Then I was really starving, so I think they starve you, but drug you so you don't know it. That's my story for what it's worth. I hope nobody else gets hurt."

Mike doubted that this was a psychotic. He wondered how Dr. Fisher could have thought she was so crazy. He had always thought that the doctor was competent and bright. Mike had been his patient for a few years while he had a general practice in town and then had sold that to establish his fat farm business. Cindy had been his office nurse during that time and had moved with him into his new business venture. It just seemed out of character for the doctor to be so wrong, but Mike was concerned that he could be.

CHAPTER 15

The more Mike Hansen thought about it, the more incredible the tale was. He must have had a blank stare as he sat at the table with Amy, Pam, and Roger. He asked her to repeat parts of the story again, mostly to give himself time to think and analyze. The more he thought, the more amazed he became. If what Amy was telling him was true, the scope of the activity boggled the mind. At least hundreds of people must have been affected, maybe more, and although most of them went home happy from the center, he could barely imagine how many laws must be being broken. If, in fact, dozens of people every month were being drugged against their will and subjected to who knows what kind of violations and inhumane treatment. It would take pages to simply write down the numbers of charges that could be brought.

Yet in an odd sort of way, it was a victimless crime. People who were overweight and unhappy paid gladly for these crimes and returned to their homes slim and delighted.

The scenario cut against the grain of Mike's past experiences with Dr. Fisher. He respected him as capable and inherently good. Perhaps Amy had an ulterior motive to discredit the doctor or his enterprise, but no motivation was evident from her conversation. There did not seem to be a personal vendetta here, at least not yet. His police training had taught him to be skeptical and seek confirmation by evidence collection or corroboration of witness accounts.

By now Mike's elbows were on the truck stop table, his chin in his hands, and he squinted as he thought while trying to pay attention to what the other parties at the table were saying. This was a real ethical dilemma. Victims of what essentially was violence being unaware of it and happy about it after it was over. It was too incredible to believe.

Was what Dr. Fisher and his cohorts were doing immoral? Probably, because the clients were subject to it involuntarily, although think of the results he was achieving. Could the outcome justify the means? Did this constitute the perfect crime? People were violated and glad that it happened. Clearly there must be risks these patrons were involuntarily assuming.

While his brain scrambled with the moral and ethical dilemma, there was no dilemma on the legal side. If Amy's story was true, laws were being broken by the fistful, and there was no question that his job was to see that it stopped and that justice was served.

Or maybe Amy really was nuts. He would have thought so except that her story was consistent with what physical evidence he had seen and settled some matters that had troubled Mike from the beginning. Specifically, if Amy's tall tale was fabricated, then how did one account for the missing horse? The hoof prints in the lawn of the house that was burglarized, the return of the pair of boots. The fact that she had taken some clothes that had not been missed could be easily substantiated if the owner identified them. What caught his attention most, however, was that she had an explanation for her lack of clothing in the first place. It had troubled him from the onset that Cindy and Dr. Fisher, who reported only that she was missing and that they had not seen her, also reported that she was minus her clothing. This incongruence had begged for an explanation in his mind since the beginning of the investigation. Not so much that an alleged psychotic would run into the woods inadequately clothed, but that somehow, Dr. Fisher already knew her state of dress.

It had also bothered him why someone who was opting to flee from an isolated set of buildings out in the country would not use their car. He now had an explanation for that too.

Three pairs of eyes with questioning stares brought Mike's mind back to the task at hand, and he realized he must have seemed absent while thinking. He apologized and explained that he was trying to connect things in his own mind. Explaining that he had a dilemma on his hands because of conflicting reports from different individuals in the case, he proposed a plan of action.

In Amy's eyes, he could see an unspoken pleading to believe her. She had laid all her cards on the table and now she would be at the mercy of his decisions. He resolved not to abuse that power.

"Okay, here's what I propose. I need physical evidence to corroborate the story. I spoke with several of the clients at the center this morning, and they gave me no indication of any shenanigans there. However, there are a couple of matters of evidence that I forgot to look for."

Hope appeared in Amy's eyes.

"If you would kindly agree to stay with one of my deputies for an hour or two while I make a search for some evidence at the center, I will return and speak with you again before any formal action is taken. We will not take you back to town yet and your presence in the valley will remain unknown until I speak with you again. Is that fair enough?"

The skeptical Roger withheld response; but Amy, who had found Sheriff Hansen true to his word so far, felt that she had little to lose with much to gain, and agreed. He spoke briefly into his radio. She thought she shouldn't have been so surprised to see another sheriff's department pickup pull into the truck stop thirty seconds after he began speaking. It impressed her that he had been that prepared. Deputy Tim, the right-hand man, was introduced to the three, and they agreed to get something to eat in the restaurant while Sheriff Hansen ran his errand.

Thirty minutes later, Mike and the doctor were standing on the deck in front of the lodge.

"I'd like to question a couple more clients, if I could." Mike said. "I only got to talk to two of the fellows before I was called away this morning."

"That would be fine," said the doctor," although all of Amy's group is departing today and some for them have already left."

"If you don't mind, I will just walk around and chat with folks a little bit," Mike said.

"Go ahead, I'll be in my office, Mike."

Thanks, Doc."

Mike walked along the rock walkway toward the bungalows. Dave and Thomas were coming out of the cabin toting suitcases. The sheriff waved to them.

"I see you're ready to head home," he said.

"Yeah, back to the grind," Thomas remarked.

"Well, you two take care." Mike extended his hand.

"We will," said Thomas as he shook the sheriff's hand. A small scab was present on Thomas's forearm just above the wrist.

"Drive carefully," the sheriff went on as he pumped Dave's hand in a vigorous handshake as well. Slightly different location, same scab on Dave, he though as he walked on past them, his head reeling. How could these people not know what had been done to them?

There was activity in the next bungalow. The Blakes and Petersons were packing up suitcases. The door was open. Mike popped his head into the doorway.

"How are you folks today?" he said in a way he thought country people ought to talk.

"Fine, thank you," said Jackie Blake. "Is there something we can do for you, Officer?"

"No, not really," he replied. "I am just here on some other business, and thought I would be friendly to the patrons."

"Now, that's nice." She smiled naively.

He stepped through the doorway. "I'm Sheriff Hansen. I just figure it's my business to nose around every place in the valley once in a while." He grinned, trying to put on an air of country bumpkin stupidity. He extended his hand. Mr. Blake took it and shook it. His hairy forearm made it difficult to distinguish anything that caught Mike's attention, but Mrs. Blake followed suit, extending her hand, and had a nice little reddened spot about a third of the way up from the wrist.

The sheriff took a chance. "Did you get in some thorns there, ma'am?" he asked, pointing. She looked down at her arm.

"Why, I don't know," she said, rubbing it. "It doesn't hurt."

"Well, I hope you folks enjoyed your stay. I best be going," he said, walking out, scanning the forearms of the remaining couple, and noting a similar mark on the left forearm of Mrs. Peterson. As he stepped out of the cabin door, he took a deep breath and reminded himself to stay calm and open minded, and he walked back into the lodge.

He took the most circuitous route through the building he could find to end up at Dr. Fisher's office, looking all the way for signs of stairwell or doorway to the basement area that Amy had described. He found nothing. He had looked over the outside of the building as he pulled up, as well. No evidence of a basement structure. The construction looked like cement slab on grade. This puzzled him, but if there was a sinister plot here, obviously they would conceal the location, or maybe Amy, in her initial drugged stupor, had confused where she was.

Dr. Fisher seemed consumed with a desire to find Amy, even under his cool exterior.

"Doc, I am spending the whole day on it today and hope to have something for your real soon. She has now been gone long enough that we can open an official missing-person's case right away."

"Thanks, Mike. For her sake, keep things as quiet as you can. I just hope she is alive and not dead from hypothermia somewhere."

"I hope so too." The sheriff began to turn to leave.

"You will contact me later, won't you, Sheriff?"

"Certainly, Doctor." And he excited.

He just had time to swing by his office and make a phone call to a police forensics lab in Salt Lake City. Mike still had a few connections in northern Utah, having worked as a deputy in the Davis County Sheriff's Department before moving up the career ladder to the job in Lincoln County.

Soon he had Fred Talley on the other end of the line.

"Fred, Mike Hansen. Long time no see. How you been?"

"Well, how you doin', Mike? Still chasing bad guys up there in the mountains?"

"Sure am. And I catch 'em too." He smirked into the telephone. "You still the mad scientist who can figure out anything?"

"Sure am," came the reply.

"Look, I do have a serious question for you. Could you take an otherwise normal person, give them drugs of some sort, put them under for a few days, then wake them up and convince them they have been somewhere else doing something else?"

"Why, Mike, it sounds like you are looking for a new hobby." He chuckled.

Mike had never thought Fred was particularly normal, but he was smart.

Fred went on, "Yes, theoretically, you could do that. And it would work some of the time, maybe most of the time. But probably not every time. Why do you ask?" "It's a long story, Fred. I just wanted to know if it is possible."

"Yeah, it's possible if you are slick enough, I suppose." "Could you guys detect the drugs?"

"Sure, Mike, we can detect any drugs." "Well, what do you want-blood to do it?" "No, urine is probably better."

"Fred, you're nuts, but you're a good buddy to have.

I will probably be calling you."

"Okay, Mike. Catch the bad guys." And he hung up. Within the allotted two hours, Sheriff Hansen was back with his deputy, his suspect, and Pam and Roger. The sheriff was careful not to reveal too much information but knew he had to entrust himself somewhat to Amy as she had entrusted herself to him if they were going to cooperate.

"I found sufficient evidence to warrant an investigation of your claims," he said to her in a businesslike way.

Her countenance brightened, and her head nodded slightly. Everybody waited for him to go on, so he did.

"We have a couple of issues to contend with here. Number one, you are a suspect in a burglary, which you have confessed to. I am sure that your full cooperation with us in these other matters can be utilized to have the charges dismissed. At least I think I have that much influence with the prosecutor. Still, we have to go through the formalities of making that happen."

Amy understood this entirely. Criminal law was not her specialty, but she was knowledgeable enough that this made perfect sense to her.

The sheriff went on. "The second issue is that Dr. Fisher believes you may have a psychiatric condition and should be held for involuntary psychiatric evaluation. He or I have the authority to require a seventy two hour observation period in jail or in a psychiatric facility if we think you might be dangerous to yourself or to others. While you seem okay to me, the doctor himself may order it. I have little control over it. Once we enter the police station, now that you have been officially apprehended, this becomes an issue." There was a brief pause while Amy's mind worked.

"Can you keep me in custody yourself for that?" she asked. For some reason, she had already developed a trust for the sheriff.

"Well, technically, yes, I can, but the only mental health professional we have in the valley for evaluations is Dr. Carl Paxton, and I suppose you might not find that arrangement very appealing."

Her understanding was immediate. "I see." She nodded.

The sheriff went on, "Amy, I'm also required to recite to you your legal rights and give you the opportunity to get the services of a lawyer."

"Thank you, Sheriff Hansen," she responded. "I understand that and will solicit services of counsel later if I feel I need them."

Pam looked across at her with an alarm and said, "Shouldn't you get a lawyer now?"

Amy put her hand on her sister's shoulder. "No, it's okay. I have nothing to hide, and I think the sheriff is trying to help me." She looked back across at Mike.

CHAPTER 16

Another half hour of elapsed time found the group sitting across from Sheriff Hansen at his desk while he filled out the paperwork regarding the burglary. He could hear voices chattering out in the front office and at the dispatcher's table. He stood, pushed his chair back, and walked out into the front. Amy could hear him saying, "I don't suppose I need to remind you all that confidentiality is important in small towns just like it is in big police departments." Amy could almost hear the heads nodding, and Sheriff Hansen walked back into his desk. By now, Roger was pretty impatient with the paperwork.

"Okay, Sheriff, where do we go from here?"

"Well, frankly, Roger, we need to think that one over. I have questioned a number of people at the center without too much success. I have some leads that I would like to pursue further. We have enough to get a warrant and search the place, but I have been through there a couple of times myself and can't even figure out where it is Amy believes she was held."

"Excuse me, Sheriff," Amy interrupted. "Aren't I entitled to one phone call here?"

"Why, yes, you are," he responded.

"I would like to make that call now, if you don't mind." He was a little shocked but agreed; she was within her rights. There was a phone down the hall that would afford her privacy. Amy responded that she would prefer he was present when she made the call and wondered if she could simply use the phone at his desk right now if it was caller ID blocked. It was. She also requested a phone book, which he provided. She thumbed through it briefly then dialed the phone.

Amy said, "Hello. Is this Rocky Mountain Restoration Center? May I speak with Cindy please?" All eyes in the room widened. She went on, "Hello, Cindy. This is Amy. I just wanted to call to apologize for running out so abruptly. I just decided to cut my stay short and go home. I guess I got a little homesick. I am sorry if it alarmed or inconvenienced you, and I am just calling to see if I could stop by and pick up my car and my things sometime." There was a pause as she waited for Cindy's reply. "Home, just planning to be at home. I hope I didn't inconvenience you. I'll make the arrangements to come and get my things as soon as possible. Good-bye." And she hung up.

Mike had to concentrate to keep his mouth from gaping as she hung up the phone. Nobody said anything. Then Pam broke the silence, lighting into her sister. "What are you doing? Those are the people who are out to get you, remember?"

Amy accepted her tirade quietly and calmly for a couple of minutes until the intercom buzzed on the sheriff's desk.

"Sheriff, call for you from Dr. Fisher." Everybody went silent as Mike picked up the receiver.

"Sheriff Hansen. Yes, hello, Doc." The sheriff's whole conversation was pauses punctuated by "Uh huh.

Uh huh, I see." Finally he impassively said, "Thanks, I will get right on it," and hung up the receiver. He looked seriously across his desk at Amy.

"That was Dr. Fisher," he said. "He says they located you at your home in Utah, that you are completely crazed with delusions that someone is trying to get you, and that he is convinced you are overtly suicidal and we need to get psychiatric help to you emergently. He advised me to dispatch an ambulance with restraints and several officers to bring you immediately to the Salt Lake County psychiatric ward under heavy sedation. He said he would call ahead to the doctor on duty to fill him in on the details of your case."

There was a stunned silence in the room as it became crystal clear to the sheriff who were the bad guys and who were the good guys in this, his latest investigation.

CHAPTER 17

As astute as Amy's action had been and as clearly as it had defined the criminals from the victims, it had left a couple of problems. Namely, she was not in Utah as she had led Cindy to believe; and, secondly, if Dr. Fisher and his cohorts found out that she was sitting in the local sheriff's office, it would blow the sheriff's cover as to his suspicions about Dr. Fisher. It might lead him to flee before the sheriff could accumulate sufficient evidence for an arrest.

Mike had to think fast. It was only moments before he proposed a plan to the rest of them. With the recent chain of events, he had now acquired Roger and Pam's complete trust, and they went along with the idea wholeheartedly. A phone call or two to Utah set things up. Fortunately, Mike's connections in northern Utah were good. Virtually all officers of the law had frequent contact with those who cared for those unfortunate mentally ill individuals whose lives intersected frequently with both the health care profession and with law enforcement. Mike had made arrangements to have Amy admitted voluntarily to a private psychiatric hospital, on a temporary basis as a cover for him to continue his investigation. At first, she had resisted this maneuver but realized that it was she who had caused the predicament. He informed her that because it was part of his investigation, the sheriff's department would pay any expenses necessary. That was the least of her concerns, however; she did not particularly want her medical record reflecting a psychiatric hospital admission, yet she realized this approach might represent the least of those evils. One way or another, they had better be in Utah pretty quick, or Dr. Fisher and Cindy would figure out otherwise. Certainly, they could feign that she had left her home in Utah and was simply elsewhere, but the fact that the personnel in the sheriff's department had seen her could not be kept under wraps indefinitely in such a small town. Right or wrong, it was a fact of life that information would leak sooner or later.

Mike helped Amy into his pickup, and Pam and Roger got into their car and returned home with the agreement that Amy would call them immediately upon her arrival in Utah to let them know she was okay. The sheriff checked out to one of his deputies as the pickup rolled out of town and picked up speed.

Despite his high rate of speed, the trip to the Salt Lake City area was several hours long. At first, both of their minds were concentrating on the task at hand, but as the relaxation of the road set in, it left some time for idle small talk between the two. Amy had started out to be Mike's suspect and now had turned into his accomplice.

"It's a pretty long drive, so as far as I'm concerned we don't have to be all business. Hopefully you can relax some."

"Thanks, Sheriff. I'll try to relax."

"You can call me Mike if you want. Except I suppose I better be 'Sheriff' in public until this is over. I'm sorry you're in this situation, but glad you are safe now, really glad."

"Well, I'm sorry to be a bother. You probably have better things to do as sheriff."

"Are you kidding? This is why I go to work every day. I chose my job hoping it would occasionally help somebody."

"That's really sweet." Amy looked down at her hands. "I don't think I've ever helped anybody, not like you, anyway." There was silence for a few minutes, but it didn't feel awkward.

Staring at the road as if in deep thought Mike said, "Your sister and Roger seem very supportive. You must get along well with them."

"Yeah, they're great. I feel lucky to have such a good family. Pam and I are pretty close. My nephew is really fun. Mom and Dad are kind of classics, funny, but real good people."

"Sounds awesome. I'd like to have cohesive family like that."

"You don't?"

"I have a sister back East, but my mom passed away. Dad works overseas most of the time. So I am just me for the most part."

"Sorry about your mom."

"It's okay. It's been a while."

"No girlfriend?" She had to know. "Or maybe that's not my business."

"It's okay. No girlfriend. You?"

"Do I have a girlfriend?" She chuckled, "No," then went on, "I'm out of a long relationship a while back. It just wasn't going to work out in the long run."

Mike nodded. "I see." He wanted to ask more but didn't want to abuse his position. "What do you like to do?"

"Oh, I like horses, but I don't have one. And camping, and good movies, but definitely not long walks on the beach." She snorted a little as she laughed at herself. "Sorry, that was headed in a wrong direction, and I couldn't figure out how to stop it."

He couldn't help but chuckle at her cuteness. "No problem, I totally got it." He thought she might be blushing.

For her part, Amy had more on her mind. Now she was going to be a patient in a mental hospital, and she had gotten herself into a fine mess. There was no longer any doubt in her mind, however, that the people at Rocky Mountain Restoration Center were up to no good. She wondered if everyone there was involved in the plot. It seemed that at least a significant number of them must be. It occurred to her she had forgotten to mention that the man and Cindy in the basement were concerned about the temperature in the place. She wondered if that was pertinent and brought it up to Mike.

He thought for a moment and said, "Sure, I think that makes sense. Their main object is to get you to lose weight, so if it is colder, your body would burn calories faster, it seems to me. I know when I am out in the back country in cold weather, I have to eat a lot more food. I'm sure that's not all from the exercise because I can climb the same mountains in warmer weather and don't get as hungry."

It made perfect sense now that she thought about it, but it puzzled her before. Her mind wandered to the imaginary scene of the sheriff in the back country. He was tall-six foot two inches with freshly trimmed thick, dark hair, high cheeks, and short squint lines radiating from his deeply set eyes. His jaw angle was sharply defined, matching his lean but muscular build. He was straightforward in his looks and his manner. She knew she felt secure with him and laid her head back to relax the last few miles before they entered Salt Lake City.

Soon they were pulling up in front of Valley View, a private, for profit, psychiatric hospital. Mike had arranged for one of his old deputy buddies from the Davis County Sheriff's Department to meet them there informally. A staff psychiatrist at Valley View used to be a resident in training at the county hospital when Mike worked for Davis County, and they knew each other personally.

"Mike, that high mountain air is good to you. How have you been?" Doctor Jim Whitney pumped Mike's hand as Amy and the two officers entered the door to the institution.

"You're not looking so bad yourself. The money must be as good as mountain air."

The doctor laughed in response.

"Jim, this is Amy." Mike had reached Dr. Whitney by cell phone en route and explained the situation that a determination of Amy's sanity, or lack thereof, was crucial to his investigation.

"Hello, Amy. We'll take good care of you here. I'll see to it personally for my old buddy." He gestured toward Mike.

Amy nodded apprehensively then she felt the sheriff's hand on her back, starting them moving down the hall.

As they walked, Mike asked the doctor to withhold commenting as to her mental status to any law enforcement or health care providers that might contact him for a seventy-two-hour period. For Amy's part, he had suggested while they drove that she simply be rather withdrawn and not say much for a while. He solicited the doctor's agreement in not pressing her for information early on to allow him time to pursue the investigation.

"Jim, I'm not asking you to compromise your ethics here. Are you okay with this approach?"

"No problem, Mikey. We've been through plenty of worse dilemmas than this before. I'll do my evaluation, keep my mouth shut, and see that Amy's well cared for and secure." He looked toward Amy, meeting her eyes. She was relieved he was so matter of fact and didn't seem to harbor preconceived notions as to her sanity.

Mike and the doctor did agree that it would be acceptable to acknowledge to those who might inquire by telephone, that she had been, in fact, admitted there, but not allow phone calls to her directly except for immediate family members and himself. Amy would call work and arrange to be absent a couple more days.

The whole thing would have been difficult to arrange if not for acquaintances and connections already existing, and Mike was grateful for the coincidence that Amy's home happened to be in the same general area he had previously worked. He knew time was of the essence, and after making appropriate arrangements and asking his deputy friend to keep an eye on the situation with Amy, he piled back in his pickup and headed for home.

He was only part way back when he thought enough time had elapsed that he better call Doc Fisher. He dialed his cell.

It didn't surprise him much when the doctor on the phone said, "Mike, I called the county hospital, and they don't know anything about Amy. Do you have any idea what is going on?"

"Yes, that's why I am calling, Doctor." The sheriff tried to produce professionalism in his voice. "The patient requested evaluation over at Valley View rather than the county hospital, and they went along with that. The deputy I talked to indicated she was there, all right, and that they were concerned about her."

"Well, is she medicated?"

"Doc, I don't know all those details. That's medical stuff. I just know she is there, and if they say they are pretty concerned, something must be wrong."

Maybe it was a white lie or bending of the truth. He did talk to a deputy. He and they-the deputy, doctors, and whoever-were concerned for Amy's welfare, so technically, it was the truth. He knew, though, that he was misleading Dr. Fisher a little to convince him that someone else thought Amy was possibly psychotic. He changed the subject so as to not divulge any more information.

"Doc, I will have to arrange some disposition for her car and her belongings. Maybe I can check with you in the morning."

"Sure, Mike, that would be fine. I am just glad they have got her somewhere where she is safe and can get proper treatment."

"Me too. I'll contact you first thing in the morning and probably bring her things to the sheriff's dispatch for impoundment."

"You're a good man, Mike." The voice on the other end of the phone went on, "We are lucky to have a constable like you to look after us."

Mike really didn't know how to respond and just hung up the phone. He stopped at a drive-in and ordered a hamburger to go. As he stepped outside, long shadows of evening gave a relaxing glow to the landscape. He had to be sure he did things right here. He felt that he had the situation on his own terms. He knew he had work to do, and he knew he had to be smarter than the bad guys, that this would be a contest of wits.

CHAPTER 18

Dr. Fisher and Cindy were together again in his office, but it was all business. It was a nice evening outside, and more for the privacy it afforded them than for anything else. He suggested they talk outside and go for a little walk. They had a big decision to make. They crossed the deck down across the lawn and out into the meadow were the creek meandered through. They, without saying much, cleared several hundred yards from the lodge. Dr. Fisher put his hand briefly across Cindy's shoulders. Although they had no relationship as such, the two had worked together long enough in both their legitimate and their illegitimate enterprises that a bond of mutual trust and friendship had evolved between them. They looked after each other. Cindy basically functioned as the right hand for the doctor's designs, and she was much better than he was at public relations and logistics. He was the idea man, she was the action woman, and both understood their interdependence on one another. They had discussed this fat farm venture many times over.

It started some years ago when after a monotonous day in the office, he had blurted out his frustrations at taking care of inconsequential things like colds and ringworm. He said, " If I could just get these idiots to stop smoking ang quit being so stinking fat, I would have done more good for them than a lifetimes worth of penicillin for sore throats and hydrocortisone for their itches." It was a legitimate frustration. Cindy's response, though, had turned an aimless outburst into something else when she said, "Then why don't you do it?" He had responded that he couldn't do it for them, that people had to do things like that for themselves, but the conversation wandered, and before long, they were kidding about taking over for people, forcing them to stop smoking and to trim down. They had joked about a concentration camp-style fat farm, where people were forced to lose weight. In a natural way, the topic kept coming up and became sort of a private joke between the two of them until eventually, the idea of profiting from doing things that were for people's own good, had allowed them to rationalize a seed of justification in what they were considering. Cindy recalled the doctor saying, "Regular weight loss clinics don't really work and there is plenty of data to back that up if you're interested. You can teach people healthy life style 'till you're blue in the face, but they don't stick to it." She had countered, "Well, what can you do differently?" "I don't know, maybe implant anesthetically modulated hypnotic suggestions during induced starvation; you know, mind control," he said, half kidding. "Is that legal?" she asked. "Probably not." "Is it possible?"

"To a degree, I suppose. It's not like I trained in it, but I might be able to figure it out."

She cut him off. "Then maybe we should do it."

Gradually, they had gotten accustomed to the bizarreness of it all and ultimately had embarked on this endeavor.

There was never any doubt that both of them knew what they were doing was wrong. Yet they were able to rationalize it and to heartily profit from it. As the concept developed, they knew they would have to bring a few other people on board. They called them the knowledgeables. They selected individuals whose lack of scruples allowed them to be purchased, and they really had had a problem-free operation until now. Now they must decide whether they would go on or give up. The financial investments in setting up their venture had been substantial. They had largely recovered those but had not yet been able to sock away sufficient for the kind of retirement they envisioned. They had almost been caught here. Did they dare continue? The popularity of their enterprise was so high that they had people scheduled for more than a year in advance. The amount of profit this represented to the two of them, boggled their minds.

This time, it was the doctor who was apprehensive. By now, they were three-quarters of a mile from the lodge, walking along the small, willowed stream bed bordered by meadows of wild grasses. The sun was a gold ball touching the horizon.

Cindy said, "If they have her in a mental institution, then haven't we accomplished just what we wanted? Her credibility will be poor; her memory is fogged by treatments. She should pose no threat. If she was really out to expose us, why would she have called me simply wanting to get her things?"

"I suppose you're right. I wouldn't expect a secretary with a blasé life to be so shrewd. If she really wanted to blackmail us, things would have played out differently."

The conversation carried on until the sun had set and dusk was upon the meadow valley floor. An orange glow could still be seen on the peaks to the east where the sunset shadow had not yet reached.

Cindy slipped an arm around his waist, gave him a little hug, and said, "Come on, I think we will be okay. We have got new arrivals in the morning, unless we bail out now."

"You're probably right. We're better off not to lose our cool. I'll call Valley View in the morning and pump the staff and then try to bias the psychiatrist. Her story will be far fetched enough to sound pretty paranoid. I'm still concerned though. We don't really have enough money to leave the country yet."

She looked him squarely in the face. "So panic on the inside, but stay calm outside-only acting worried will give us away." She was always the stronger one.

He shrugged and agreed, and they turned back toward the lodge with the conclusion that they had made Amy look crazy enough they could proceed. There had always been an element of risk in what they were undertaking, and always would be.

CHAPTER 19

The next morning amid the hustle and bustle of new arrivals, Sheriff Hansen came out to the center and collected Amy's car and her belongings. He spoke briefly with Dr. Fisher, who had called Valley View Hospital and confirmed that Amy was there and being taken care of. What he didn't tell the sheriff was that he had tried to extract information regarding the psychiatrist's clinical impressions of Amy but that they maintained their professionalism and did not divulge. This did not surprise the doctor, and he had momentarily satisfied himself that records of a psychiatric hospitalization following her running away was sufficient to discredit her. He also had an evaluation report from Carl that now had been rewritten with remarks about unstable behavior and paranoia. Furthermore, no blackmail had yet surfaced. It was, for now, back to business as usual.

Mike again walked the grounds and building since they were allowing him more or less free run of the place, but he could not figure out the basement area where Amy had reported being held. He dared not ask too many questions of the staff because it would best suit his interests if no one was suspicious that he, himself, had suspicions. By afternoon, he was scratching his head. Then an idea occurred to him.

One o'clock found his gray pickup parked next to a new red pickup with the door reading R & B Construction. The sheriff hailed two carpenters clad in tool belts, scrambling over roof rafters as they applied plywood to a framed structure. These guys were some of the busiest and best contractors in the valley and had made a good business out of residential construction. They were occasional fishing buddies of Mike's and about the same age.

"We didn't do it, Mike," yelled Hal down from the roof to the lower story, his muscles flexing through his T-shirt as he positioned a four-by-eight, three-quarter-inch plywood sheet. He picked up his air-driven nailer, securing it in place with deft strokes.

"I should have been a carpenter," retorted Mike, his face turned skyward. "Have a new pickup, tack a couple of boards together, then fish the rest of the week." He grinned.

Not to be outdone, Hal responded, "Well, get rid of that goofy cop suit and grab a hammer. We could use the help." He clambered down from the rafters, leaving his coworker up above nailing. He dropped from the ceiling joist to the floor smiling and said, "So, Mike, you ready to let us build you decent housing? No woman is going to take up with you living in that place, you know.

Mike stepped a couple of steps closer so that only Hal could hear him. "Say, didn't you guys do most of the construction on Doc Fisher's fat farm?"

"Well yeah. That was a job we were glad to have because it was big, kept us working for a long time."

Mike went on, "I just want to prod your memory a little bit about a basement in that place."

Hal said, "Yeah, that foundation is really screwy under there. The architectural specs were for extra deep footings, which left a crawl space as big as a basement. We told the doctor if he was going to pour that much cement, he might as well use the space and build a full basement, but they told us they didn't want anything below grade. Doc said something about earthquake resistant footings or something. I have never seen anything like it though."

Mike pulled Hal to the far end of the building, intrigued by this and wanting to be sure that only Hal could hear. "Tell me more about it," he went on. Hal said, "What is the interest, Mike?"

"I just need to know for professional reasons," he went on, and his look conveyed the seriousness necessary that Hal understood that he needed to know. Reaching in his belt and pulling out a carpenter's pencil, he squatted down on the subflooring, sketching lines.

"See, here's the lodge layout. Do you know where that deck comes off the front at floor level? That's all backfilled dirt up there. It used to slope away, but the footings were so deep with so much concrete exposed that it was ugly, and when we got finished, they added the deck, mainly to cover that up. The main fireplace in the lobby sits on a concrete pad something like nine feet deep. It serves as a main support from which over-sized footings run like walls in all directions. We also poured vertical slabs every twelve feet for floor support across the whole width of the building," he said. "It must have cost them a ton of money, and I don't know for what."

"Hal, is there a way to get down in there?"

"Well, sure, there is a crawl space access-there has to be by building codes," he said. "We kept trying to tell them they ought to just make a basement down in there, but it was all broken up by those walls every twelve feet, not much usable space, maybe for storage. He did have us pour a stairway down into it, but in the end, they didn't want to use it and there is just a crawl space access through the subfloor back in the kitchen. We built a wall right across the top of those stairs we poured."

By now Mike was incredibly intrigued. "Where do those stairs come up?"

"They rise toward the back as I recall," Hal said. "That main hallway where you go out of the lodge on the south side toward the bungalows is where they ended up. I think there is storage rooms all along there. A lot of that is kitchen. Why, Mike, what are they doing, running a poker game in the basement?"

"No, not exactly, Hal, and you know I can't tell you what's up. You have been a lot of help. Can you sketch me a more exact location?"

"Well, I don't remember it in a really detailed way, but that stairway will be behind a wall in one of those storage rooms along that back hallway. If there wasn't a wall there, you would see it, but we sheet rocked right over the top of that, I am sure."

Mike could barely believe what he was hearing. He thanked Hal and said if he ever wanted a real job, he could quit this building business and come be a sheriff's deputy. He climbed in his truck and took off.

CHAPTER 20

It was Friday night. Amy looked at the walls in her room, blank but for her television, and marveled that she was a patient in a psychiatric hospital. True, they had treated her well enough, but she wondered what all this was going to accomplish. She'd heard nothing from anybody, although she called Roger and Pam frequently. They had agreed to continue to keep the matter a secret from the parents. Pam called her folks and mentioned she had seen Amy and so her parents had no cause for alarm. They suspected nothing and assumed she was back home by now. Surely her parents were interested in how she had fared, but Pam had put them off by saying Amy had indicated she would call them in a few days. Still, here she was in another hospital gown in an institution, which was more or less how this whole thing started out. She alternated between scared and bored and was half-disgusted with herself for going along with it. She couldn't believe how bizarre her life had become.

A nurse rounded the corner into her room and said, "Amy, you have a visitor. Do you want to see somebody?"

She was immediately concerned. She had actually thought that maybe Cindy would show up and strangle her in her sleep in order to silence her. When she had these thoughts, she wondered if she really was crazy and maybe Pam, Roger, and the sheriff had simply used an alternative argument to convince her to be here because somehow they could tell she was nuts.

"Who is it?" she asked.

"He says it's Sheriff Hansen. He has a badge."

"Okay," she said. "What do I do?"

"Put on your robe and come down to the visitor's lounge," the nurse replied matter-of-factly.

So she did.

As she rounded the corner into the lounge, there was Mike Hansen. No Smokey the Bear hat this time, just his normal head of hair, and it had been combed too. He was in his civilian clothes, jeans, and a cotton duck shirt. He looked very nice, holding in his hand a bouquet of flowers. A warm smile dressed his face.

Amy was surprised.

"Hi, Amy. I thought you might be lonely."

Actually, she was, and he was a welcome sight. He stuck out his hand holding the flowers toward her and she took them.

"Flowers?" she questioned.

"Sure, aren't you supposed to bring people in a hospital flowers?" he said and continued without a pause, "Since I know the top brass around here, I have made arrangements for you to have a little leave of absence and go have dinner with me tonight. Do you suppose you could stand being out with a country boy like me for a couple of hours?"

She couldn't help but smile. He was trying to be cute, and she liked it. Her acceptance of his offer obviously pleased him. He said, "That's a pretty darn nice robe you have got on there, but if you would rather wear something else, I could wait a few minutes."

She almost giggled as she nodded and hurried back to her room to find some clothing. She didn't have much to choose from because she had been left off with only what she had been able to bring from Pam's. She had some slacks and a blouse and a pair of shoes and hoped that he would understand.

As they walked out the front of the hospital, he extended his arm, and she took it in her hand. He led the way out into the parking lot where not much to her surprise, was a pickup truck, not the police one, but his own apparently. It was a dusty tan color trimmed in black with aggressive-looking tires and wheels, but not overdone. It had a short bed and an extended cab with a little seat behind the main seat. As he helped her in, she found hazel eyes staring at her from under quite a bit of fur.

Mike said, "Oh, I would like to introduce you to my buddy Max. He's my roommate and gets lonely when I am gone a lot, so he asked if he could come along for the ride. I hope that's okay. He promises to be good."

She reached up and patted the dog on the head, and he in turn explored her hand with his nose. She thought the whole thing was kind of cute. She was definitely not out with one of the smooth, citified professional that she was more accustomed to dating. The pickup was new and still had that new car smell. Mike came around and climbed in the other side.

"Now you behave, Max, and don't be licking the lady," he said. The dog lay down obediently on the back seat, and they rolled out of the parking lot. Any felt so refreshed to be outside of that hospital and wondered how people who had extended hospital stays managed to keep their sanity at all. She had this big rush of freedom come over her, and she realized how pleased she was to be out or maybe it was that she was pleased to be with Mike.

He looked over at her and grinned. "This is your town, ma'am, so you are going to have to find us a place to eat 'cause the only restaurant I know here has golden arches." He snickered.

"I know a good place up in the university district," she answered.

"Sounds great. Give me directions." He looked over at her. "You look real nice."

"Thanks," she said, patting her hair conscientiously. "I don't feel nice. I feel pretty horrible."

He reached out his hand hesitantly. "Are you hanging in there okay?"

"I am," she replied, studying his face. "But it sure feels good to be out of there and with you," she said with a quick downward glance.

"Glad to be of service." He responded with an exaggerated nod.

As the evening wore on, however, there was some business to be transacted. Mike had come to trust Amy completely, so he shared with her the findings so far. He was thoroughly convinced her story was true; he simply needed to establish it sufficiently to apprehend the perpetrators. He had to question Amy a little about the goings-on in the early days of her stay because he didn't want to barge in too soon. With a new arriving group of clients at the center, he wanted to time his response to catch Dr. Fisher and his compatriots in the act of a crime. He told her about Hal's description of the staircase and asked her to try to recollect where she was in the center. By the end of the discussion, both had pretty much concluded that she had come up to the top of the stairs through one of those storage areas and out the hall to the south side of the lodge. Mike was convinced he had it figured now.

One of his nagging concerns was what to make of the photograph of Amy playing volleyball or of Dave holding his big fish with his fishy-smelling clothing that had to be laundered. If one was comatose in a cold room in a basement somewhere, it would be difficult to have yourself photographed fishing or playing ball.

Ultimately, the two colluded to continue the investigation, and Amy agreed to stay where she was for the time being. Mike was convinced it was safer than returning to her home because if the stakes were as high as he thought they were, it was best to let Dr. Fisher think that she remained psychiatrically incarcerated.

It had gotten late, and Mike had agreed to have her back to the hospital. He had arranged to stay with his friend in Davis County and dropped Amy off. They climbed out of the pickup at the hospital, Amy giving a friendly farewell to Max who was happy for the company and the doggy bag he had received. She gave Mike a little squeeze in the doorway of the hospital and then went in.

The next morning, Mike climbed out of bed in Davis County and called Fred Talley at home.

"Fred, your buddy Mike Hansen. Are you up yet?"

"It's Saturday, Mike, of course I'm not up."

"I thought good scientists never slept," he said. "I'm sorry to call so early, but I've got to head back and wondered what you had found out on the urine specimen we sent over from that Amy?"

"Yeah, that's really interesting," he said. "I just finished it up last night. I guess you knew that. She's got a regular pharmacy in her."

"What do you mean, Fred?"

"Well, there are at least six drugs in there, so what-ever she has been doing, it involves a concoction of things. Funny stuff for somebody to be taking on their own though."

This didn't surprise Mike. "Yeah, so what's in there?"

"Well, there is ketamine that one will put you to sleep for a long time. They use that on horses."

"Do they use it on people, Fred?"

"Oh sure, it gets used some for anesthesia. There is a bunch of benzodiazepines in there too and some traces of some atropinic agents."

"Good work, Fred," said Mike. "Now tell me what you really just said.

"Well, basically, what's in her is some combination of anesthetics. I'd say if you wanted to slip somebody one dandy of a Mickey Finn, this would be the way to do it, but these drugs, or some of them anyway, can't be taken orally. They would have to be administered by injection somehow."

"Are they controlled substances?" Mike responded.

"Oh, absolutely. Hospital use only, most of them," he said.

"Thanks, Fred. Record that as evidence. I think I will be needing it. I will be in touch."

"You're welcome, Mike. Keep up the good work, and for Pete's sake, stop calling me on Saturday."

Mike pretty much had it put together now. He called Amy just long enough to tell her that the investigation was going okay and that he had enjoyed being with her. He asked if it would be okay if they tried that again sometime. She said she would love to but would prefer to be picked up at her home instead of at a mental institution and that it might be better for his reputation anyway. He agreed wholeheartedly as they had a little laugh together. He made his way home as quickly as he reasonably could in a non-police vehicle.

On the way, he reviewed the entire case with Max, who with careful consideration agreed that he was on the right track.

CHAPTER 21

In a calculated fashion, Mike waited until Sunday afternoon before taking any further steps. From what Amy had told him, there would be a period of adjustment and activities at the center before the comatose weight-loss program began. He was concerned about letting Doc Fisher start another session, but he felt like he needed it to make his case. In any event, they had apparently been going on like this for several years, and no one had died. Still, if they barged in on the situation, he knew he might need medical assistance, so he arranged that through the state forensic medical department. By Sunday evening, he had gotten together with Tim, his deputy, and confidentially explained his findings so far. He had kept this investigation largely to himself because of its sensitivity but felt like someone else in his department needed to be in on it in case anything happened to him.

Monday morning, he checked with the State Board of Pharmacy and the local hospital. Controlled sub-stances had to have records for interstate commerce, and he was unable to find sufficient documentation to explain an extensive amount being present in their locale. This further confirmed his suspicions that illegal interstate commerce of controlled substances was going to be yet another allegation in this case.

By Monday midday, he was at Rocky Mountain Restoration Center. "Just checking in," he said to Dr. Fisher.

"Thanks, Mike, I appreciate this." The doctor asked about Amy, but he betrayed himself in the conversation such that Mike could tell he had been checking with Valley View to make sure that she was still there.

Mike asked what people were up to today and made the remark that he didn't see too many people around.

"Well, a bunch of them are floating the Snake River and some are out on horses and others out for a jog. Why do you ask, Mike? Are you still interested in enrolling in our program?"

"Well, that depends how good the fishing is on the Snake," Mike said.

"Usually pretty good. They get some big ones once in a while," responded the doctor.

"Yes, I suppose they do," said Mike. "Do you fish mostly above the elbow?"

"Yes, always above the elbow, Mike, that lower section's got too rough of water for some of the greenhorn clients we have."

Mike acknowledged that he should have known that himself, and it was good of the doctor to be so careful. "You say there's a group up there today, huh?"

"Yes, there is, Mike," said the doctor.

"Well, if they do any good, I might call you to find out, because I would like to know what the fish are takin'." He kept his country bumpkin facade up as well as he could and then finally left the center.

He stopped at home, switching into his private pickup and swung by Tim's place, who was also off duty. Tim had a fourteen-foot, flat-bottom aluminum boat that was ideal for floating that section of the Snake River, which was known for its excellent fly fishing. Mike had, as soon as he had gotten home, called Tim and instructed him that they were going to be going fly fishing that afternoon and to get his boat ready. They went as civilians, although Mike carried a handgun in his gear bag. They went to the elbow, dropped off one vehicle, and put in further up river. Mike fished this area fairly regularly and often fished with Tim, so it was not unusual for the two of them to be on the river. Tim knew this was not actually a fishing trip from their previous conversation; and so as Mike, Max, and Tim settled into the boat, they made a few half-hearted casts but mostly made rapid headway down the river. They passed occasional other boats. Each time they approached one, Mike reached into his dry bag, pulling out a pair of binoculars, and glassed it carefully. As they rounded one bend away from the road, they pulled over into the shallows. With the binoculars, Mike studied for a moment and then said, "Tim, grab your rod and start fishing."

Tim understood and made obligatory casts. Through the field glasses, Mike could make out a party of individuals with a boat pulled to the bank. People, arranging themselves in various ways, and a photographer snapping pictures, which would not have been unusual on a river where large fish were caught, for people were prone to take pictures of their catches. However, as Mike watched, he noticed a very interesting operation.

A snap shot or two was taken with poles in hand, and then people reached into their boat, pulled out different clothing, changed clothing and hats. He was pretty sure he could make out someone slipping on different hair, and then more pictures were taken.

After he had satisfied himself this was the charade of pictures he thought it was, he and Tim pulled their hats down, donned their dark glasses, and floated as inconspicuously past the group as possible, making casts with their fly rods as they went by on the far side of the current. Sure enough, both Mike and Tim recognized Ted, the photographer. As they got to the end of the float at what was called the elbow of the Snake, they also recognized his vehicle, so they loaded their boat and quietly waited in another part of the camp-ground away from the boat dock, but where they could sec. Shortly thereafter, Ted and his entourage in the boat floated into the area. They loaded the boat on the trailer attached to Ted's land cruiser who got in alone and drove away. The rest of the group then all retired to their separate cars and departed separately. Tim and Mike followed at a safe distance behind Ted, back down the valley to the Rocky Mountain Center.

None of the other vehicles went to that location. Ted had an inordinate amount of gear he had loaded into his vehicle, and so it was no surprise to Mike when he later called the center and the desk person reported the Snake River group hadn't come back yet that evening. It was a foregone conclusion that these were not fishermen, but models.

This left a nagging concern as to how Dave had a picture of himself with a great big fish and, not only that, had the fish to show for it when Mike had talked to him. It was easy enough how they could make the peoples' clothes smell like fish, but Dave himself took home that big trout he bragged about.

There was only one option, the local trout ranch run for those too inexperienced to catch a wild trout. You could go fish there and pay by the inch for the fish that you caught, some of which were gigantic. He knew the owners. A phone call confirmed that Rocky Mountain Restoration bought fish from them.

"Not only that," the owner said, "the funny thing is the little fish are better eating, but they always buy the big ones from us. And they won't take any with damaged fins or skinned noses. They're sort of particular, I'd say."

That was all Mike needed to know. This solved the last great mystery. For when he had talked to Dave and seen his big trout, something was wrong. The Snake River only had cutthroat trout, not rainbows. Besides, no fisherman catches a six-and-a-half-pound trout and doesn't know what kind of fly he was using. As a matter of fact, no respectable fisherman would forget in his lifetime what kind of fly he was using when he caught a trophy like that.

That night, Mike and Tim met at the sheriff's office to review the information and the charges they would likely bring. They determined the interstate violations they expected to confirm, would necessitate Federal Bureau of Investigation involvement.

They planned their strategy and returned home. Mike called Amy to fill her in on the goings-on.

After explaining the plan to her he said, "I think we can get you discharged from that place tomorrow as soon as the warrants are served and arrests made." He paused. "I hope the end of this case doesn't mean the end of seeing you, though."

"You'd better see me," she retorted. "Or I will be jay-walking right in front of the police station and you'll have to take me into custody."

"Duly noted." he said, shaking his head as he smiled broadly.

"I was thinking maybe I should be up there tomorrow. You know, to identify things if you needed me to."

He didn't need her for that and he knew it, but he said, "That's not a bad idea. But I have to be here now."

"Maybe Deputy Tim could come get me," she replied. "Just get me a leave pass like you did before."

Mike thought, Women are so shrewd, but he was powerless to resist the temptation. "I'll call Tim and see what we can do. Call you back real soon."

CHAPTER 22

Tuesday morning dawned beautiful, bright, and warm. It was summer in the mountains. Things were pretty quiet at Rocky Mountain Restoration Center since most of the clients were in a peaceful, drug-induced sleep, in their cool cubicles. Lawrence was there picking up horses that had been used a couple of days before. Ted was constructing photos, along with his helpful AI program, and Cindy busied herself about her endless organizational activities. Dr. Fisher was finally feeling relieved that they had skated by a close call and had survived. He walked out on the deck to take in a long drink of the morning.

At the end of the center's lane, three sheriff's department pickup trucks and two state highway patrol cars turned off the paved highway and proceeded up the drive at a brisk rate of speed, leaving trailing dust in the crisp morning air. The doctor's mood changed immediately. He sprang for the door of the lodge, barked to Cindy, and pointed down the road. There was no other road out, but there were the mountains. He went into his office and opened the closet next to the file cabinet. He procured a short-barreled shotgun and a small backpack that were stored there. Cindy stood immediately behind him. The two had a contingency plan to leave the others and escape to the mountains. They both spun in unison, exiting through the back hall onto the back lawn where a thumping sound made them look up to see a black helicopter with the letters FBI on the side settling toward them.

The doctor yelled, "Come on!" and sprinted toward the face of the slope.

Cindy, apparently taken by the chaos, hesitated only momentarily, but that was enough for two men in SWAT gear to jump from the landing chopper and overtake her as she began to run.

Mike saw the capture as he rounded the corner of the building. Judging from Cindy's trajectory he deduced Dr. Fisher was ahead, probably taking the horse trail through the pines. His instincts told him Doc would try to make it over the top of the big main ridge east to the heavily timbered drainages on the other side. It was a no roads wilderness area and would be easier to hide in. This was confirmed as one of the federal officers pointing, yelled, "He's armed!"

Mike took off in pursuit, knowing that to run up the trail behind his fugitive would readily give him away as the fleeing man would be watching behind. Mike was younger and somewhat taller so he banked that his athleticism would let him gain elevation cross country despite having to scramble through the dead fallen lodgepole that littered the forest floor. He went hard and fast, straight up for two hundred yards then cut right, toward the horse trail he knew. His hunch accurate, as he struck the trail Dr. Fisher was looking down, struggling to keep his footing on the steep face barely below Mike.

"That's far enough, Doc," he said, his breath coming hard. His hand went to his holstered .41 magnum revolver as he saw the shotgun. He did not draw, hoping to avoid escalation, but looked to a tree trunk to his left for cover if the shotgun was deployed.

Startled, the man looked up the slope for the first time. "You gotta let me go, Mike."

"Can't do that."

By now the doctor was gesturing in Mike's general direction with the shotgun. "I'm serious, just let me pass."

Mike had been in this situation before, but it didn't make it easy. This was a man that he had already misjudged, but he proceeded, "You're not going to kill anybody."

"I'm pretty sure I can hit your leg from here," was the quick reply.

Mike stood his ground. "We know everything. It'll go better if you don't make me draw this .41."

"Mike, I was doing what was best for these people."

The sheriff replied, "I understand. I do. But you got it all haywire, Doc. You'll get plenty of chance to explain it, I expect." He took a step forward toward the still shotgun pointing doctor.

Instinctively the doctor stepped back, catching his heel on a deadfall at the trail's edge, which sent him catapulting over the log downhill. As his hands reflexively reached to break the fall, his grip on the shotgun was momentarily lost.

Mike reacted instantly with two long downhill strides and a dive toward the doctor who was frantically reaching for his weapon. Unfortunately, Mike's dive was not as clean as he would have preferred, his right knee smacking against the log. This in turn slapped his head to the deadfall, skidding his face along the bark as he ultimately did clear the obstacle, his momentum carrying him pretty much on top of the doctor. Mike succeeded in batting the shotgun away from the struggling man, and before the scuffle was over the federal cops were there. Gasping in the high elevation air, they had the doctor, spitting pine needles, in their grasp.

Mike laid there a moment longer, contemplating the pain is his knee.

"You all right, Sheriff?" one of the FBI men asked.

"Yeah, banged my knee. I'll get up in a minute," he answered as the agents ushered off the hand-cuffed suspect.

The sheriff remained on the ground catching his breath, then determined to get to his feet. He rolled prone, pushed up on his arms and briefly evaluated the crunchy sounds his right kneecap made. Drawing his left leg under him in order to stand, he heard something and looked down the trail. Ever faithful Tim came into view just below. Amy was right behind, or more like passing him as she saw Mike on the ground. By the time he could awkwardly rise to standing she was there, pressing into him.

"Are you okay?" she yelped, wiping at his bloody check with her hand.

Calm on the outside, his penetrating eyes saw the glistening perspiration on her forehead, the panic in her face, her belabored breath. She was beautiful all a tizzy.

"Are you okay?" she persisted.

"I am now," he said as he slid his arm around her panting shoulders. "I am now."